PRAISE FOR *THE SORROWS OF OTHERS*

"Every once in a while, a new writer come   perceptive, empathetic, and intelligent that i   with
the form all over again. The relationships   ll of
quiet ardor and tangled duties; at the hea   vorld
rendered with care and skill. *The Sorrows*   najor
literary talent, one anyone who loves reading should experience."

—ARNA BONTEMPS HEMENWAY,
AUTHOR OF ELEGY ON KINDERKLAVIER

"In these marvelous stories, Ada Zhang writes with ferocity and precision about feelings
and situations I have seldom seen captured in fiction before: a woman caring for the
dying husband who has abandoned her, a girl glimpsing what her grandparents have
endured in China. Each story offers a deeply satisfying world, one I never wanted to
leave. *The Sorrows of Others* is a brilliant debut."

—MARGOT LIVESEY, AUTHOR OF THE BOY IN THE FIELD

"These stories contain a rare and profound understanding of loneliness, in all its ges-
tures, nuances, and variations: the loneliness of aging, of being othered, within families
or in solitude. Above all, Ada Zhang has captured the essential loneliness of human
interiority, the experience of being alone in one's mind. Every story is written with
grace and a light touch, scenes subtly washed with feeling as a skilled watercolorist
floods a landscape with color. A wonderful debut."

—KIM FU,
AUTHOR OF LESSER KNOWN MONSTERS OF THE 21ST CENTURY

"To read Ada Zhang's collection *The Sorrows of Others* is to be in sublime relationship
to human follies and to wisdom and to the silence that is cultivated between lines and
after a story ends. This is a collection to savor and to reread."

—JAI CHAKRABARTI,
AUTHOR OF A PLAY FOR THE END OF THE WORLD

"Each story in *The Sorrows of Others* is elegantly braided and brushed with a careful
hand. This debut collection resists the temptations of flash and clamor, embracing a
more modulated, substantial prose that resonates richly, with a deep understanding
of character and of true mystery. Prepare to be ushered into the everyday fascinations
of the various lives depicted here, and prepare at each story's end to be left wondering
and aching."

—JAMEL BRINKLEY, AUTHOR OF A LUCKY MAN

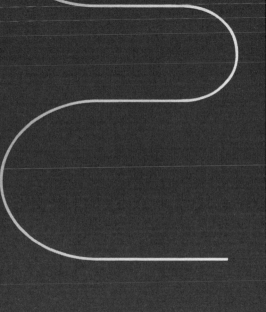

The Sorrows of Others

The Sorrows of Others

Ada Zhang

A Public Space Books

A Public Space Books
PO Box B
New York, NY 10159

Stories from this collection appeared, in earlier forms, in the following publications:
"Compromise" in *A Public Space* No. 29
"Knowing" as "Goldfish" in *Alaska Quarterly Review*
"The Subject" in *American Short Fiction*
"Sister Machinery" in *Catapult*
"Any Good Wife" in the *Rumpus*
"The Sorrows of Others" in *McSweeney's*
"Propriety" in *Witness*

A Public Space gratefully acknowledges the support of the National Endowment for the Arts, the New York State Council on the Arts, the Amazon Literary Partnership, and the corporations, foundations, and individuals whose contributions have helped to make this book possible.

Library of Congress Control Number: 2022942307
ISBN: 9781736370964
eISBN: 9781736370971

www.apublicspace.org

9 8 7 6 5 4 3 2

*For my aunt, whose love endures
distance, language, and time*

谨以此书献给我的大姑姑，
她的爱跨越了时间，空间，语言和文化。

You don't have a home until you leave it
and then, when you have left it, you never can go back.

—James Baldwin, *Giovanni's Room*

Contents

The Sorrows of Others

The Subject

The summer before my junior year, I moved out of the dorms in Baxter Hall on the corner of Broadway and East Tenth and took a room in a small house on Cherry Avenue, Flushing, Queens. I told my friends it was to save money, and they didn't ask why I didn't move to Brooklyn or Long Island City. Anywhere would have been closer. I suppose it was a point of pride among my college friends to live frugally even if it was selective. Even if it was abstract, since it was our parents' money we were spending every time we went out, our parents who paid our rents. But we were all very young back then, and I regarded hardship the same way I regarded my own shadow. I was aware of it but rarely thought of it. Either way, it did not frighten me.

The house was a low, squat rectangle with a patchy yard and a maroon awning over the front door. The windows were barred. A chain-link fence wrapped around the house, separating it from the sidewalk and from the homes on either side, which looked more or less the same as ours, the two-bedroom I shared with Granny Tan: red brick with asphalt shingles scaling the roof, all faded and curling around the edges. At parties that summer, my living situation lent me an air of authenticity. I'd recently bleached my hair and dyed it blue to make up for the fact that I did not grow up in a progressive household. My parents are Chinese immigrants. We were middle class. Their politics were what you might expect. They believed in taxing the rich but not in affirmative action. At the time, this brought me a deep sense of shame.

"I live in Flushing," I would tell a room full of hipsters, most of them art students like me. They all stepped closer. "My roommate is this old Chinese lady."

"How old?" someone would ask.

"In her seventies I think."

"Why does she need a roommate?"

"To save money I guess," I would say, and shrug. "Same reason as anybody else."

The hipsters would nod and drink their beers, smug in the idea that there was a real one among us. There was a palpable fear in every young liberal back then that one could never be poor enough or of-color enough to outweigh whatever privileges one had. Even those on scholarship felt insecure. We talked our heads off about gentrification but said nothing when friends moved to Bushwick or Ridgewood, the then up-and-coming neighborhoods. It was amid such confusion and self-loathing that I began searching for a new place to live.

I loved Flushing because I chose to be there, but at the time I believed I loved it for different reasons. The food, Chinese restaurants all up and down Main Street, noodles and dumplings next to Thai restaurants, Korean, Vietnamese; and the people, who looked like they could be my relatives, the aunts and uncles and cousins I saw once every three or four years. We lived close to the botanical garden where it was quiet. I figured that was why the streets had such names as Maple, Blossom, Dahlia, Elder.

I wanted to be an artist. A painter. It requires a certain amount of idealism to make art, and that comes more easily to some than others. The more privilege you had, the more ideal you ought to be and the more you should be expected to suffer; that was what I thought. Portraiture was a dying form—and still is—but I decided that if I was going to make a name for myself, painting faces was the only way. It was political and also romantic, my desire to suffer. It served me well while I had few responsibilities.

I took a job at the bubble tea shop next to the Flushing station, making twelve dollars an hour scooping tapioca balls inside a shoebox that fit three customers at a time. I didn't need the work, but it felt in line with who I thought I was becoming. At night, in the blue darkness of my room in that house, with one fan blowing on me from the nightstand and another rotating around the room, I wrote my obituary: "In college she lived in Flushing, Queens, the last stop on the 7 train, in a predominantly Chinese immigrant community.... She lived prudently and apart from distractions, so she could focus on her art...."

I used to recall fantasizing about death and cringe, but not anymore. Now I think how lovely it is that even death was dressed in the glamour of my dreams.

Granny Tan was short and wide, with brown skin that was crumpled all over but nowhere so much as her face. Her hair was like a rain cloud, white at the top and dark near the scalp. She kept it in a tight bun that frizzed from the humidity that was particularly bad that summer, small hairs springing from her head like the whiskers on a roused cat. She left every morning in a pair of pink Adidas slides, holding a broom in one hand and a dustpan in the other. She picked up napkins, MetroCards, chip bags scuttling around on the street, as well as trash stuck inside our fence, candy wrappers and other miscellaneous scraps woven into the silver fishnet, paper cups jammed into the holes, suspended in the shapes of diamonds. She wore gloves and a surgical mask while she worked. Afternoons she went out in tennis shoes, collecting bottles and cans from our neighbors' trash and carting them to the redemption center on Maple Avenue, a twenty-five-minute walk away.

She ignored me, not out of rudeness or even indifference but because she had her routine and wouldn't let anyone disturb it. Contrary to my apprehension around living with someone much older, she wasn't fussy about the apartment, nor did she try to assert her dominance over what had previously been her space. She didn't own the house but had rented it for twelve years, first with her daughter and then with her grandson. I didn't know any of this when I moved in. I learned it in the months following, when I interviewed her for the project that would turn into my senior thesis.

What I did know:

1. There was a woman named Sharon, who'd posted the Craigslist ad and to whom I paid rent.
2. Subletting was technically not allowed, and while this seemed sketchy to me, I also saw it as an advantage. I could rent month to month and leave whenever I wanted.
3. There was a boy. He looked about five or six. His photo, showing wet lips and missing teeth, stayed taped onto the refrigerator.

The photo was a personal detail in an otherwise anonymous home. All the furniture was the same color, brown, and the carpet was so off-white it was beige. I wanted to ask about the photo, but Granny Tan was always so busy. For weeks it seemed I scarcely saw her beyond our polite greetings in the living room, either at noon when I left for my classes in the city or in the evenings before she went to bed.

"Is the landlord paying you for the work you do?" I finally asked on our first real night together. I'd been in Flushing for six weeks. I was conducting the first of our many interviews.

She scoffed. "Na li, na li. I just have nothing else to do. I'm old."

"Shouldn't old people rest?" I had heard the neighbors advising Granny Tan to take it easy, but at this she laughed, a hoarse wail that fell quickly into a cough, and I worried I had somehow offended her. She cleared her throat, then leaned forward so her chin was nearly touching my phone resting between us on the table. "It's recording, right?" She lifted her head so that our eyes met. I told her that it was, and that she didn't need to be so close for it to catch the sound, but she just hunched lower.

"Listen to me, ah, young people. Don't spend your time wisely, as many will try and tell you. Wisdom is for people like me, who are old, who are trying to make up in utility what we've lost in time. Be frivolous while your body and spirit can keep up." She nodded and smiled, as though affirming herself. Through the open windows, the vague melody of Mandarin drifted in from our neighbor's CCTV.

I wanted to know what Granny Tan was like when she was young. Instead I asked what picking up other people's garbage had to do with wisdom.

"It's a wise way to use one's time, don't you think?" She leaned back in her chair, a peeling leather office chair on wheels, which made her look strangely official. "Time slows when you're by yourself. It gets harder to feel useful."

I was just thinking that she wasn't by herself when she asked, "Why do you paint?"

"It's a way of using my time too, I guess." I was hoping to win her favor.

"Do you enjoy it?"

"It's my passion," I said.

"Then perhaps it's frivolous as well."

Hold on, let me get closer. Okay. Ask me again.

How long have you been retired?
Two years, technically, if you don't count what I do now as a job, even though some days I'm busier than when I had a paycheck. I worked at a nail salon. I had to stop because of my eyesight and my shaky hands. It's detailed work, painting nails, and depending on the customer, it can get very intricate.

Intricate how?
There are all sorts of details, flourishes, but that wasn't the hard part. People are paying you money to pay them attention. That's what it's really about, that's the exchange, not the nails. People come in needing to feel cared for. The streets need to be cared for, too. You wouldn't believe how filthy they get! Anyways, that was my job, but it got harder once my eyes and hands started going. My boss was a kind lady. She kept me on for as long as she could. My daughter still works there. She's been there for as long as I've lived in this house. Twelve years.

It sounds like you enjoyed the work on some level.
Of course. I find pleasure in whatever it is I'm doing. If I hate something, I can't expect to do it well. It's the same for most people, I think. I believe excellence is a basic human desire.

That's optimistic of you. What were you doing before you came to the US?
I delivered babies. I was the midwife in the village where I lived. It's what my mother did, what her mother did before her. Our family trade, you could say. I always knew it was what I was going to do. I saw my first birth when I was nine years old. Would you like to have kids one day?

I'm not sure.
Well, don't wait until you're my age.

How many babies did you deliver?
I've lost count. There's nothing like a baby's first cry. I never got used to the sound. It's the mother who's doing all the work. Pushing and pushing, until her face is as red as a sweet potato. But from the crying you'd think that the baby emerged out of the sheer force of its own will, its determination to be part of the world. Wahhh! Wahhhhh!

Do you miss it?
Miss what?

Being a midwife. Delivering children.
You seem to associate things a lot with emotions. Talking about liking this and missing that. It's just work. I do what I have to do to the best of my ability. It doesn't bring me great anguish, nor great joy. It's a livelihood. It's not love. Then when it's time to move on, I move on.

I would like to tell myself now that I was interested in Granny Tan for who she was. She was compelling to me, and the paintings and interviews were a way for me to get to know her, that was what I'd thought, but what ended up happening tells a different story. The portraits I did imitated three of the most well-known portraits in the world: *Girl with a Pearl Earring* by Vermeer, Kahlo's *Las dos Fridas*, and of course, the *Mona Lisa* by Leonardo da Vinci. I painted in acrylic. The integrity of the replications was in the positioning of the subject and nothing else, no frills or tricks, I didn't try emulating the artists' styles. We recreated the poses at night in the living room with all the curtains drawn, using a single naked bulb for light.

"Like this?" Granny had said, twisting her neck to face me.

"Perfect," I said, and snapped a photo. "Just like that."

At the senior gallery, one of the things people talked about the most was the light. One person, a stranger, said this was most striking in the homage of *Las dos Fridas*, where two identical Granny Tans sat side by side holding hands, and the light spilled from both faces, as though emerging from within.

Experiences and fun are for the young. Understanding is for the old.

Can you say a little more about that?
What more is there to say?

Tell me about something fun.
Summers in my village were very hot and wet. I guess not so unlike how it is here. One day, my friend and I had the idea to steal a watermelon from my neighbor's yard. It was risky. We knew we could get in a lot of trouble. I'm not sure what made us want to do it except that we'd heard her brother and his friends bragging about stealing one before. I guess we thought if they could pull it off, why not us?

How old were you?
Ten, eleven.
We waited until dusk then snuck into his yard. He was a very skilled grower, this Uncle, and watermelons were his specialty. We pulled the first one we saw and ran off with it in my shirt. We couldn't go home, so we went to an area where farmers took their sheep. My friend had a pocketknife. She cut around the melon and then dropped it on the ground so it split into perfect halves. We ate using our hands. We got lucky it was so red and sweet. We raised our melon halves in a toast before drinking the juice at the bottom.

You got away with it, then.
When I got home I was in trouble for staying out late, but no one noticed my sticky hands. No one ever found out it was us. But we felt

so guilty about it afterward we decided we could never do anything like that again. I don't regret it though. Everyone should do something like that when they're young, when the consequences for things are small. If we'd been caught I would've gotten a serious spanking for sure, but I would still have this memory. I haven't stolen anything since.

Where's your friend now? Are you two still in touch?
She lives in our village still. We send voice memos every now and then, but I haven't been back since I left.

That was twelve years ago.
Yes, and I know what you're going to ask. Do I miss my friend. Ha!

Do you?
I think of her often.

If you could see her now, what would you say?
I would say… I know what I would say. I would say: Qiu-ah, we're old now. No one can spank us. Let's steal another watermelon!

By November we'd had our first snow. When I came home from class one day, Granny's daughter and grandson were visiting. They'd just come inside. They introduced themselves as Sharon and Ricky, the rent collector and the boy on the fridge.

"It's nice to finally meet you," said Sharon. She was thin and tall and looked nothing like Granny Tan. We shook hands limply. Hers was very cold.

"You can speak Chinese," said Granny, helping the boy as he wriggled out of his coat. "She understands."

"Really," said Sharon, seeming more at ease with me. She ran her fingers over her son's hair. "That makes me hopeful for Ricky. He's been speaking English more to me ever since he started school."

"My mom had a rule growing up," I said, "that we could only speak Chinese in the house. If I asked her something in English, she'd ignore me."

"You must have been a very obedient child," said Sharon, smiling. She was pretty. I had trouble picturing her doing nails. "I don't know if I could get Ricky to do the same."

"Ricky, can you tell jiejie hi?" said Granny.

"Hi," he said, making a show of it by letting his head fall back. He looked older than in the photo. His face was darker and less round.

Our evening interviews continued every other weeknight, always in the same place at the same time, in the kitchen around seven. December was when I began noticing a shift. Granny started dropping in on me randomly throughout the day whenever I was home, which was more often now that it was getting colder. She would knock on my door and say something like, "Have I told you about the time I stole a watermelon?" or, joking, "I found a watch today on the sidewalk. You want it?" and we'd end up chatting off the record for an hour, an hour and a half.

Before finding it unbearable, I must have enjoyed it. On some level it was what I'd hoped for, Granny Tan seeking me out. It wasn't abnormal roommate behavior. She would go on about Ricky, his struggles in school, apparently he was having trouble reading; about the homeless people at the redemption center with bags five times the size of hers. Close to the end of my stint on Cherry Avenue, she would bring up a saying in Chinese—"What's the point of living in a golden palace when it's full of shit?"—explaining for what felt like the hundredth time why it was important to her that our street remain nice-looking: it was named for a flower. That implied that it aspired to beauty.

I must have told her some things too, I forget what, but after a few weeks, I began dreading her knock on my door. If she were a friend I might have set some boundaries, asked for a little space, but I never viewed Granny Tan as a friend. That much is clear to me now. She was old to me, and I pitied her more, having less respect for her as time passed, even as I found her life worthy of art.

The Revolution affected the whole country, so it definitely affected me. I'm sure your parents too. They must have told you some things.

We don't talk very much.
You should just ask them questions like you're asking me.

Granny, do you mind if we stick to the script tonight? I'm pretty tired.
Fine, let's stick to the script.

How did that period affect you specifically?
In the turnover between Chairman Mao and Deng Xiaoping, when the revolution was ending, there was a lot of change. The country was trying to build itself up again. You can see how we were successful in that, by the way. Just look at China now. But my job got more complicated after the one-child policy. I want to say here on record that it was a good policy.

You don't have to say that.
But I mean it. The whole country was close to starving at one point, we were all eating cornbread that tasted like chalk, but now look. Everyone's rich! It's common sense. With fewer people, there's more of everything to go around.

What about the people in your generation? Who will support all of you as you get older?
Our government.

Governments don't care about people. They care about power. That's true in every country.

Of course you'd say that, living here where even idiots feel special just to have an opinion. How would you explain China's rise in the last twenty years?

You were talking about the one-child policy.

Right. The policy was strict. There was absolutely no leniency. We all knew that any woman pregnant beyond her first child would be subject to a forced abortion. We aborted at all stages of the pregnancy, even the final trimester. Some of the fetuses were fully formed when they were cut out. I didn't perform the operations, to be clear. Trained medical professionals from the city did that. I just assisted in the clinic. I was a midwife. My job was the opposite of theirs, but I had to show my solidarity with the policy, you understand.

Did you ever question the policy?

No, not really. Although some nights when I couldn't fall asleep, my thoughts would naturally drift in that direction. There was one woman who managed to hide her pregnancy for seven months. Her belly was swollen to the size of a watermelon by the time she was brought in. She cried and kicked, cried and kicked. You should have seen her. She was strong. She did everything she could to get away. It took me and three nurses to hold her down. These things never feel right in the moment.

They feel right to you now?

Many women went through the same thing, and the country is stronger now because of those sacrifices. So looking back, it was right. It didn't feel right, but it was right.

What was it like being a midwife at that time?

I saw a few women more than once, and I always had to ask what happened to the firstborns, the girls. I had to be sure I wasn't complicit in breaking the law.

What happened to them?
Those women?

The baby girls.
Oh. Gotten rid of somehow. I didn't ask for details. From the looks on the mothers' faces, I knew they were telling the truth.

How do you feel about sons versus daughters?
Boys carry on the family name.

But you're a woman and you have a daughter.
Do you have a boyfriend?

No.
Someone you're interested in at least?

Why are you asking me this?
Well you're young, but eventually you'll want someone to provide for you and protect you, and the sooner the better. Don't wait till you're my age!

Your daughter will provide for you and so will Ricky.
They have their own families to think about.

What are your hopes for Ricky as he grows up? Do you have any?
Only that he's healthy. And that he's not too serious. My daughter was too serious. I want him to enjoy himself.

What if he turns out to be different from what you expect?
I expect him to be different.

What if his views don't align with yours?
They most likely won't. The lives that you and I have lived, and that me and my grandson will have lived by the time he's your age, are worlds apart. You have your ways and I have mine. He'll have his. We believe what we've learned in order to survive. I wouldn't take that away from anyone.

Before Christmas that year, the cold had turned bitter. The 7 stalled more than usual, or maybe it just felt that way because the sun set so early and my entire commute was cloaked in darkness. It took an hour and twenty minutes for me to get home, and while that never bothered me before, it started to. I began spending less time in the city. I attended class but skipped social invitations, and while my friends used to come to Flushing now and then for dim sum, by then the novelty had worn and they preferred staying close to campus. I saw pictures of them online, sprawled in each other's tiny rooms. They would stumble into class together wearing sleepy smiles, holding matching coffees, late despite living nearby. I was annoyingly alert by the time I arrived and also exhausted. I quit my job at the bubble tea shop just to have one less reason to go out.

The street we lived on was unplowed. I walked in the sooty snow to avoid stepping on ice. The apartment was poorly insulated. Granny kept her puffy jacket on indoors and was still leaving twice a day for her routine, but this no longer struck me as remarkable. Our neighbors kept telling her to stay in, reminding her of her age, how she could slip or catch a cold, but she wouldn't listen.

"Please," I said to her one morning, stopping her at the door. "At least wait for the day to warm up."

"I'm wearing many layers," she said, and stepped past me.

She'd told me before, I can't remember now if it was during a formal interview or not, that in the winters in her village, she worked in the frozen rice paddies barefoot to avoid trampling the crops. She got cuts that bled all over her ankles and feet. I watched from the living room as the wind whipped snow all around her, like giant plumes of smoke.

This country cares too much about Black people and homosexuals.

Where did you get that idea?
I read the news.

What news?
The Chinese news. Last year, when that Black man was shot. Why did the Chinese police officer go to jail? All those white police officers in the same situation and they didn't go to jail. If you ask me, this country discriminates against Chinese.

You should be asking why those white police officers didn't go to jail.
There are too many different people in this country. It's hard for people of different backgrounds to agree. That's what I told my daughter, but she didn't listen. She married a Muslim.

And that's bad?
It's easier to be with someone who comes from the same place as you, so you at least have the same starting point. You can agree on basic things.

Was your marriage easy?
No marriage is easy. I left my husband, as you know. At the last minute, he changed his mind about coming here. He was a man who valued his comfort, he was never good with change. He passed up many good opportunities just to stay comfortable. I did what was necessary for me and my daughter. What's going on with you and your parents, by the way?

Nothing. We just don't talk much.
Why not?

Whenever I talk to them I end up feeling bad about myself. I'm
sure they feel the same about me. It's easier not to talk.
What do they say that makes you feel bad?

They think I'm critical of everything. They don't agree with my
politics. The last time I saw them, they told me they don't like
my hair. They think my natural color is better.
Well that's true. The blue doesn't suit your skin tone.

They don't like it because it reminds them that they don't have
control over me. They also don't like that I chose a school so
far away. Or that I'm majoring in art.
Maybe they like you as you are. They don't think you need to change.

You don't know them. They're going to get a divorce any moment,
and they should. If it weren't for me, they would have separated
a long time ago. They fought constantly while I was growing up.
The three of us were always miserable. Every time following an
argument, my mother would do the laundry. She washed everything.
Clothes, sheets. I knew to stay out of her way. This one time I
was twelve. I was in the shower and when I turned the water off, I
noticed blood running down my legs. I'd gotten my period once
before, but the blood still scared me. From the upstairs bathroom
I called out for her. My father was asleep. I kept calling and calling
until my throat hurt and I was crying. Later she asked me why I
didn't come find her sooner, but for some reason going downstairs
seemed more impossible the longer I stayed in the bathroom. Part
of it was I thought I couldn't move because of the blood and because
I was naked. But I think part of me just wanted her to come to me.

But she came eventually.
No. I wrapped myself in a towel, stuffed some toilet paper down there, and went downstairs. She was putting clothes into the dryer. From the look on her face when she saw me, I knew she'd heard me.

What was the look?
Guilt. She looked really sorry. I told her my period came, and she immediately fetched everything I needed and put clothes on me like I was a toddler. I was already feeling better, but I stayed quiet so she would keep on being nice to me. She cut up some kiwi from the fridge and dried my hair while I ate. It's the closest I've ever felt to her. After that, she and my dad didn't fight for almost a month. That was what it was like. If I somehow got injured or sick, or if I was having trouble in school, they could put their differences aside. But if I was fine or happy, they could have killed each other.

None of this sounds extraordinary. It just sounds like an ordinary family, an ordinary marriage.
I have a headache, Granny, I'm sorry. Let's stop for tonight and pick back up later.

I don't think your parents should get a divorce. Divorce is never necessary.
You say that but you left your husband.

That's different. We had a chance to come here. At the last minute he changed his mind. What was I supposed to do?
*   Have you ever painted your parents? You should paint your mother drying your hair.*
I'm not interested in my parents.

You're interested in me for some reason, and I'm practically a stranger.

The house began to feel small. When I first moved in it smelled like camphor, and it concerned me that after five months I could no longer detect any scent at all. I sniffed my clothes self-consciously.

The winter was passing less idyllically than I'd imagined. I was painting a little in my room but mostly watching reality TV and eating whole bags of Bombay mix in one sitting. The starch gave me stomachaches. Granny would barge in and ask how the painting was going, glancing at the empty easel and the three canvases facing separate corners, the dried paintbrushes scattered. Her question felt like a stab, even though I knew that wasn't how she meant it.

"Just let me see," she said more than once, playfully, but I could tell there was part of her that really did want to see. Who wouldn't want to see themselves depicted? But I knew how she viewed me, as idealistic and young, and I withheld the paintings as a way of maintaining some authority.

"You'll see once they're finished," I said every time.

I made sure my door was locked when I wasn't home.

I blamed her because I was stuck with her, and as punishment she received my reticence. It was around then that I began to want to leave Flushing, which meant that I was living there for the first time. Our evenings together stopped. I felt like I had to be in my room now, to guard the portraits. When a friend of a friend reached out looking for someone to live with, an apartment in the city subsidized by her parents, I figured I had suffered enough. It was a deal I couldn't turn down.

"I leave at the end of the week," I said to Granny one afternoon. We were in the kitchen at our usual place around the table. "I'll pay for the next month so you have time to find a new tenant. I should apologize for my moodiness lately," I added sheepishly. "The commute to school has been hard. My new place will be a lot closer."

"Good," said Granny, without missing a beat. "You're right to make things easier on yourself."

"You should make things easy too," I said. "Stay inside. Read or do something that doesn't make you trudge around in the snow."

"It's my time," she said benignly. "I'll spend it how I please."

During the medieval period, portraits functioned much in the same way as photographs today, their purpose being to pick up where memory leaves off, so that a person could be present at a distance and remembered long after their death. Portraiture's first subjects were kings, queens, and other members of royalty. The faces painted, in other words documented, were the faces of people with power, wealth, and prestige.

The subject of my portrait triptych is Female, Immigrant, Elderly, Unmarried, and Unemployed. These intersections place her in the narrowest margins of American society. She comes from a rural village on the outskirts of Xi'an, China, where she worked as a field laborer and a midwife. For the past thirteen years she's lived in Flushing, Queens, where she enjoys keeping her neighborhood clean and redeeming plastic for five cents a bottle.

When you look at these portraits, I hope you'll ask yourself: What is nobility? Does it have a skin color, a gender, a class? When we make art, what are we saying about legacy? About memory? And if to be loved is to be remembered, then who is worthy of love? Why?

The Vermeer homage is my favorite now. I love how youthful Granny looks there, with the conspiratorial glance over her shoulder. It must have been how she looked the first time she stole. I don't paint anymore, but if I did, I would add a fourth portrait, an original. That was what my project was missing. I would paint Granny's face the way I saw it when we lived together, the way I see it now when I close my eyes.

It's after she knocks on my door. Her head is poking in. There's something she wants to tell me.

Back in the city, I smoked cigarettes and went to parties. I hung out with hipsters and dyed my hair purple after the blue faded. By the end of the school year, the portraits were done, but something still felt off. Our interviews had been intended as source material just for me, to help inspire the paintings, but I was worried people would find my project lackluster or incomplete, so I got the recordings professionally translated. On the day of the senior showcase, I set up a small TV with headphones next to the triptych on the third floor of the art building, so people could listen to snippets of our talks. For non–Chinese speakers, which was most people who attended the event, English subtitles flashed on the screen.

My parents flew in for the show. They were the only ones who asked afterward what Granny Tan was doing now, and I told them she still lived in Flushing when the truth was I didn't know. A year after I moved out, I still had Sharon's email and invited her family to the gallery but never heard back. It made me wonder if Granny said something to her about our final conversation.

That afternoon, I was shocked she wasn't asking me to stay. She had told me so much. I'd thought we'd grown close. But there was no way I would have stayed, even if she'd asked me. Perhaps it was my guilt about this that made me pick a fight.

"Why doesn't Sharon visit you more often?" I asked. "Why do you never go see her?"

"She's busy. I told you the boy's father and I don't get along."

"They can't just leave you here on your own." I felt myself getting riled up. "That's cruel at your age, even if it's to save money."

"We're not saving money," Granny said. "We're making money."

I waited for her to laugh, but she just blinked at me. Her face held no expression.

"We overcharge on the room, your room. I was sure you'd already guessed that."

I asked how much they were overcharging. She said an extra five hundred a month above what they paid to the landlord. I turned away from her and stared out into the living room, feeling lightheaded. The brown furniture swirled as the carpet tilted. Everything began caving in.

"Your daughter leaves you here so she can pocket five hundred dollars a month off a stranger."

"Five hundred is a lot to us."

"It's illegal," I said.

"The money is for Ricky."

She said this without apology, merely offering an explanation. She zipped up her puffy coat and frowned. Her skin was so deeply engraved.

I stared at Ricky's photograph on the fridge, counting three missing teeth.

"Why are you telling me this now?" I asked.

She leaned forward like she did during our evening interviews when it was dark, even though it was early then and bright out, a rare clear blue sky visible through the window. There was no phone between us.

"I've never lied to you," she said.

"You stole from me."

"I've always answered all your questions."

The Sorrows of Others

The apartment was eerily clean, and he wondered if she had not been trying to restore the place so much as to make it foreign to him. Surfaces shone. Fruit, which he always let sit in plastic bags, now rested decoratively in a glass bowl. Even useless objects in drawers, trinkets and receipts that had somehow accumulated, were given their own containers, shallow jewelry boxes that she had presumably collected over the years and brought with her to her new home. She had been there for only one night, and already he had to ask her, his new wife, where to find his lightweight coat, his materials for calligraphy, the small spoons he liked for his tea.

"You sit," she said to him, getting up from the couch where she was reading a newspaper. He saw when she put it down that it was one from last month. "I'll get it."

Before he could object and say that the tea had already been made, that he just needed to know where the spoons were, she was off. Her steps were small, he noticed, and quick, slippers clapping evenly from the living room all the way to the kitchen.

When his daughter had called a month earlier to say she had found the perfect match—someone he might connect with, since the woman happened to be from his hometown—his reaction had moved from shock to humiliation. He had no idea that his daughter had been searching, or that his current situation was a problem that needed to be resolved.

"I'm fine on my own," he'd said to Xiao An, following a silence on the phone.

"She's never been married," she replied. "In her forties. Parents dead. No kids. Also, you're both from Changwu, so you'll already have something to talk about. I'm telling you, Ba, even fate couldn't have come up with someone better."

"I don't understand. How did this come about?"

"A matchmaking agency called Planet Love, for people middle-aged and older. I made you a profile. Ba, don't be prudish," Xiao An continued when he was quiet. "Everyone goes through a matchmaker these days. The young, the rich. Everyone's looking for love."

His daughter, whom he affectionately called Little Comfort, had been motherless since she was two years old. She possessed a determination that she got from neither him nor her mother, and every time she sensed an opportunity, she was quick to snatch it up. She had moved to Shanghai for college and had been there ever since. Twice a year she came back to Xi'an to check on her father, and to complain to him about the rigors of life in a Tier One city: the housing market, construction, supermodels and actors walking with their noses up, as though the whole city stank, which, she added, it did. She compared it with the relative ease of Xi'an, which was still considered Tier Two, though they both knew that with tourism on the rise all over the country, the imperial capital was also changing.

Songhao had a humbler attitude toward risk, harboring the superstition that only if he rarely took chances would the world occasionally give him what he wanted. His first marriage to the woman he'd loved was his prize, he'd thought, for living cautiously, until one day his young wife died of an aneurysm in her sleep. After that he stopped believing in his formula, but his aversion to risk grew harsher. He stared at his dead wife's photograph once a month, keeping it in the drawer of his nightstand where he also stored the watch she'd given him on his twenty-sixth birthday, at the beginning of their love, which ended up being not far from the end.

His sole ambition now was to live a quiet life, not to disturb others or be disturbed. He'd remained single for the past thirty-two years. Another person could only bring complications.

"What does she want out of marriage?" Songhao asked his daughter. "Does it say anywhere in her profile?"

"It says she wants a roommate to whom she can offer her sympathy," Xiao An said. "Not exactly the most exciting plea for romance, but that's all she put."

"I've rearranged, I think you've noticed," Yulan called from inside the kitchen, as though having read his mind. Without thinking, Songhao had taken her place in the center of the couch. Realizing he was sitting in her warmth, he scooted over hastily. "You'll tell me," she said, "if I've gone too far."

She emerged with the tea on a tray and sat across from him on the other side of the coffee table. He watched as she poured the tea confidently, as though this had been her apartment all along and he was just visiting.

"Not to worry," he said. "The mess was fine for a bachelor, but not suitable for two. Everything is much better." He picked up his cup to hide his face, embarrassed at his readiness to please, a quality he'd always despised in himself.

"Wait," she said. "Have some honey."

He liked his tea bitter, he was going to say but was too slow. She had already opened a small jar next to the teapot and was dipping a generous serving into his cup, using one of those little spoons that he liked and that he still did not know where to find. She stirred until the amber had dissolved, and the spoon—she tapped it twice, on the edge of his cup—came out clean.

"Honey has a lot of healing properties." She set the spoon down on the tray. "It's good for digestion and regulating body temperature. We need those things as we get older."

He would have found her irritating were he not impressed by how in control she appeared in her new setting. Her movements were swift yet not at all hurried. Her profile on Planet Love revealed that before this, she'd been living with her sister in a traditional home with two rooms, a kitchen, and a small courtyard in the center. The information was on the third page of her profile, behind facts about hair color, face shape, face pigment, shoe size. It had comforted him that he could picture how she lived, since the home he'd grown up in had been similar. He and Yulan were both from Changwu, that was true, but his daughter had overlooked the more compelling coincidence that they were also both from Yaertou, a compound within the village. It was this detail, discovered on their first and only meeting, that had brought his old superstition back. He'd agreed to the marriage, wondering if it wasn't fate at work after all.

The café where they had met was dark. Yulan happened to be in the city visiting a nephew and had reached out to Xiao An the night before. They might never have met otherwise.

"People leave home seeking change," she had said, when he'd asked why she never left. "But to me, home is where you experience the most change, should life bid you stay. People go, new people come. Buildings are demolished and rebuilt, or abandoned. Children grow up. The truest change, the kind that changes you, happens when you don't choose it."

The fact that she was choosing to leave Yaertou now was not lost on him, but he didn't ask further questions. He hadn't been back there since his parents passed, but as if it were an etching in his mind, he could picture the four-hour bus ride that Yulan had taken to get to Xi'an, having made the trip many times when he was in college. The apple trees, then cornfields, then wheat fields, the world opening wide like a mouth before being siphoned into the throat of skyscrapers, smog, traffic, advertisements, the city. Yesterday they had met in the office of civil affairs. They were married in under ten minutes and afterward took a taxi back to his apartment, where Yulan got straight to tidying up, refusing the cantaloupe he sliced as well as his offer to take her out to dinner. It wasn't late, but she told him to get some rest, as though he were the one who'd made the long journey.

"You know, before you, I hadn't met another person from Changwu, let alone Yaertou, in many years," he said now. "Funny, isn't it? How we never know when our past and present might meet."

She smiled, revealing one crooked gray tooth on the top left. She wasn't bad-looking, he decided. There was a girlishness in her round face, and she was neither thin nor fat, just sturdy, a body that paired well with her manner.

"It is strange," she said. "What might be even stranger is that I have memories of you, from when you used to come back. I was a girl. I doubt if you would remember me."

He was jolted by this framing of their seventeen-year age difference. He was sixty-one; she was forty-four. If they had married years ago, when she was in her twenties, they might have raised eyebrows, spurred judgments, but now no one would even look twice at them on the street. His wife was younger, but not young, and he was old. They were both past the age when people worried about their potential losses.

"Drink your tea," she said. "Don't let it get cold."

He took one long sip, then another.

"I know that your first wife passed away unexpectedly. You labeled yourself a widower on Planet Love, but I remember you from when you were married. Your wife was gorgeous, and so modern. I was twelve when the news got around...."

She spoke faster.

"People talked about it because you were sort of a big deal, one of the first from Yaertou to be admitted to a university. My mother always told me that if I studied hard, I could be like you, I could get out of the village and be in the big city. It was a long time ago, but I think it's only respectful that I offer my belated condolences."

Something about the way she said the last part—with her head down, occasionally flicking her eyes up at him—felt like an invitation. It was his fault he hadn't prepared for this. Privacy wasn't prized where he and Yulan were from, a community comprising only ninety families. He'd gotten too comfortable in his solitude, protected by the anonymity of sharing a city with over eight million others.

"It was a long time ago," he said, "but now that we're talking about it, I remember you too."

It was a lie. He had no memory of her at all, had trouble even conceiving of her as a child, but the least he could do was try to match her sense of their familiarity. He kept on lying. "Your face hasn't really changed."

Her gray tooth showed again. "A lot of people tell me that."

"What is Changwu like these days? It's bigger now, I imagine."

"In the countryside it's mostly seniors. Young people either live in the township or have moved away. My favorite of my sister's children just moved to Shenzhen for college. Your daughter lives in Shanghai, right? What does she do?"

"She manages musicians at a record label."

He repeated some jargon that Xiao An had thrown at him over the years, but the truth was he wasn't exactly sure what his daughter did. She traveled a lot and was always too busy to provide a proper explanation. But Yulan seemed satisfied. She nodded with her mouth open, and he felt relieved that they had moved into more pragmatic territory. It seemed like they were hitting a stride.

"Do you like the tea?" Yulan asked. "How is it with honey?"

"Good," he lied again. "Good."

He woke up from his afternoon nap to find his books in the living room newly shelved next to the television. The glass case, which held Xiao An's old toys and some souvenirs, had been dusted and wiped down. It caught the glare from the sun. The items now sat gingerly against a backdrop of spines, angled so they complemented one another.

The colorful and intentional display gave an upbeat quality to the room. He felt only slightly exasperated that he'd gotten used to his scattered stacks, that he could point to any surface and say what book used to be there, having created a system out of his disorderliness. He'd long ago memorized where in the apartment the floors creaked, what type of clicking came from the radiator versus from the walls compressing and stretching at night. But seeing how different everything was, he felt suspicious that his home, now, would betray him.

To make sure he was alone, he called out Yulan's name.

No one answered.

"Yulan?" he called again.

Back in his room, he shut the door silently and phoned Xiao An. She answered on the first ring, but it was loud where she was; they had trouble hearing each other. He tried speaking again once it got quiet but became seized by a cough. He sat down on the bed. Xiao An asked if he was okay, her concern sounding too close to pity.

He'd called to tell her about the spoons. They'd been a gift from Xiao An a few years ago, a six-piece set she'd brought back from London. Instead, he asked what she was up to.

"We took some clients out to lunch. The restaurant is packed. I'm in the bathroom."

"I've bothered you at work."

"It's not a big deal."

"Next time don't pick up."

"When did you become so considerate? Is everything okay? You didn't knock your head, did you?"

This was closer to their normal rapport, but the pity was still detectable. Why else had he called, if not to receive pity? Yulan had done nothing wrong, yet here he was, acting like a child, ready to tattle on his wife to his daughter.

"Everything's great," he said. "Yulan has been reorganizing. She's completely transformed the place."

"Good. It desperately needed a makeover."

"What if I can't do this, Xiao An?"

"Do what?"

"What if I'm too used to being alone?"

Songhao knew it was because his daughter loved him that she had signed him up for Planet Love, because she loved him that she had sifted through so many women's profiles, looking for someone who could cook and clean and who might need a man just enough to find a retired chemist attractive but not enough to exploit his modest government stipend. Marrying Yulan was his way of accepting Xiao An's love, but he had hardly considered the practical benefit for her, how it would only become greater as he aged. Every time she came home, she teased him about some new habit he'd picked up, walking around with glasses perched on his head or, the latest, pitching his entire torso forward to sit. But it was true, his eyesight was getting worse. One day he might need the anchor of another person to help lower him down.

"I don't want to be someone's burden," he said, not sure whom he was talking about anymore.

"You raised me by yourself." Her words came with a small echo. "Was I a burden to you?"

"That's different," he replied.

"How so?"

What had happened to Xiao An to give her such a functional view of companionship? She'd had boyfriends before, but none of them was ever serious enough, or so she'd said, to be worthy of an introduction. Maybe he would have taken Xiao An's mother for granted had she lived long enough for his feelings to wane and grow, eventually taking a familial shape. He still loved her for who she was when she died, someone separate from him and therefore incomprehensible.

When Xiao An was growing up, other parents attributed her precociousness to being motherless, saying that it had made her perceptive and sweet, but Songhao didn't like how that discredited his daughter's natural abilities, meanwhile implying that goodness came from tragedy. Goodness came from goodness, he'd tried to teach Xiao An, by giving her the most carefree childhood he could imagine. The two of them fed ducks at the park every weekend until she was eighteen, a tradition they reprised now and then, passing a stick of candied hawthorn between them by the water. But she was an adult now. She should have the kind of love he'd had, even knowing how things had ended.

He felt hopeful for Xiao An, which made him happy. As with any true happiness, grief was there along the edges. His daughter should be open to love, young love, but that required being open to pain.

"You should get back to your party," he said to her.

"I have a few minutes."

"There are errands I need to run."

"Liar."

He could tell she was smiling.

"Fine," she said. "But let's pick a date for me to visit soon. Give

Yulan ahyi my best and tell her I look forward to meeting her."

He waited for her to hang up, but Xiao An didn't end the call. He sat there, listening to the sounds of the restaurant, picturing his daughter in her life, until he heard footsteps at the front door.

As the weeks went by, Songhao observed Yulan rearranging his schedule just as she had done with his things. On his own, he'd come to depend on his routine, the way it salved the daily task of passing time, but with Yulan the days passed quickly and without much effort, so while it was unsettling at first when she would suggest doing something new, after a while he didn't mind following the trail of another person's decision-making. Calligraphy moved to before bed so they could take a walk together in the morning. His tea was shifted to noon. On Tuesdays and Thursdays, their walks were combined with tennis racket aerobics in the park, an activity they picked up by chance one morning after a woman offered to let Yulan borrow her racket. Yulan turned out to be excellent; she was also younger than everyone in the group by at least ten years. She stood at the edge and completed the motions with a forcefulness that made it look like she was playing real tennis, slices and backhands at an invisible ball, while the rest of them, including him, looked as if they were square dancing with paddles.

Yulan took Xiao An's old room while Songhao continued sleeping in the bed he'd shared with his first wife. It was the only place in the apartment that was still his, that Yulan had not touched. At first this comforted him, but soon it made him uneasy, and he would hold off going to his room until he was on the very cusp of sleep, nodding off while brushing his teeth. Sex was never a question. He'd been grateful and horrified, upon reviewing his own Planet Love profile, to see that Xiao An had checked "Not interested" for him. Yulan had checked the same. He was curious whether his daughter viewed him as inherently sexless but had neither the courage nor the indecency to ask.

By week seven, spring had turned to summer and they had firmly established their places in the home. After lunch, he stayed at the table reading a book while Yulan sat cross-legged on the couch with her newspaper. It was never the paper of the day but an old issue, as though it took a month or two for the news of the world to ripen into Yulan's own personal tragedy. A talented young biochemist poisoned by jealous peers; a stabbing on a train; a woman who stomped a kitten to death in high heels in a video that had gone viral. Yulan expressed these miseries to him every day over dinner, as they sat facing each other at the table that separated the living room from the entrance.

"Another building collapsed," she said to him one night, holding her bowl and chopsticks limply, as though in presentation. "In Wenzhou. Twenty-two people died. Did you know?"

The news had made international headlines weeks ago, cited as the deadliest case of building collapse that the country had seen in recent years, ever since these ramshackle tofu houses started popping up all along city perimeters, providing shelter for migrant workers.

"I had no idea," he said, keeping his gaze low. "What happened?"

"There were four buildings. They were put up quickly, and no one enforced construction codes. The buildings collapsed at three in the morning. Can you imagine? One second, you're getting a glass of water or going to the bathroom, thinking you're at home, you're safe. The next second, the ceiling falls, the ground slips away, and you're dead."

He imagined the scenario as Yulan described it but would never have if it weren't for her insistence. He did not possess her ability to see the likelihoods of other people's lives.

"A three-year-old survived the crash," she said. "Her father shielded her from the impact. He was one of the twenty-two who were found dead."

Her head had sunk between her shoulders. She hadn't touched her food. He couldn't understand what it was like to feel this deeply for strangers, but he supposed this was a way to stay afloat on top of loneliness, buoyed by the sorrows of others. He thought maybe that was how she'd remained on her own for so long, and why she had picked him out of all the bachelors on Planet Love, because only a longtime widower could understand her propensity to sadness.

"You should eat," he said, and pinched a bundle of mustard greens into her bowl.

"I'm not hungry," she replied.

A few times since moving in, Yulan had casually brought up his first wife, always flicking her eyes up at him like she had that first morning. While he knew that, as a couple, they should be able to talk about their pasts, he was feeling more and more like he didn't want to. He wished to keep his heartbreak close, not let it enter the torrent of all the world's misfortunes, which were infinite, as Yulan had proved over the weeks, no one more special than the rest.

She set her bowl down and moved to the couch.

"I can bring the food over to you," he said from the table. "If you would like."

"No, that's all right. You go on and eat."

She grabbed a newspaper from the coffee table shelf, an issue so old and worn that when she opened it, it didn't make a sound.

Something caught his eye. Above Yulan's head, next to the south-facing window, was a group of framed photographs that had always been there, of him and his daughter at various moments in her childhood—birthdays, graduations, the zoo—but now there was a new picture, hanging on its own above the others. His glasses weren't nearby. He squinted to see the photograph of his first wife, the one from his bedside drawer.

Yulan had gone into his room. When?

How many times had he stared at that photo? Hundreds, probably. Her eyes, as bright and as unassuming as they'd been on the day she and he first met, when they were students at the university. The photo captured the thoughtless smile of someone for whom death felt so far away, it was basically impossible. Songhao blinked. Beneath his first wife, Yulan's head moved back and forth as she scanned the page, searching for another story.

Yulan couldn't take away his sorrow, but in living with her, he thought perhaps there was a place for it. His sadness and privacy complemented her sadness and openness, and in that way, each person had nothing to hide. They could be themselves.

Songhao turned back to his food and reached in. The pork and vegetables were delicious. Tomorrow, he decided, he would go to the newsstand and buy as many newspapers as he could carry home in his arms, current editions and back issues. If anyone asked, he would say they were a gift for his wife.

Propriety

I wanted something basic. A swimsuit that covered up what it was supposed to, with no greater aspirations. Functionality over style, I had decided, and that's exactly what I told the sales guy when he asked what I was looking for.

It was the middle of May, and already the Texas heat was unbearable. In the weeks leading up to graduation, Natalie and I would cut eighth period to go to the pool. "You still have to do well on your finals, Jiajia," my mom kept saying, but even she knew that my efforts now wouldn't amount to much. Yale had rejected me, and I was already making housing arrangements in Providence where I would be attending Brown in the fall.

He was short, all lean muscle. He wore a tank top with tan joggers and walked with an affected limp. In front of the women's rack he told me about the buy-one-get-one-fifty-percent-off deal, and as I flipped through the padded bikinis and strappy one-pieces, he lingered to say that my freckles reminded him of Lucy Liu because she was also Asian with freckles. On my way out empty-handed, he asked for my number. I put it into his phone, saving my last name not as Xu but as Lucy Lookalike. He promised to hit me up soon.

A week later, as I was setting the table for dinner, my phone vibrated.

Plans tomorrow?

I texted back, *Who is this?*, sure that it was that guy. I'd forgotten his name. "Who is it?" my mother asked, placing soupspoons in bowls.

"My friend," I told my mom, glancing at my phone as it shivered again. Then read out loud, "Collin."

"*Col-lin.*" She said his name slowly, feeling the syllables in her throat, on her tongue. "A white boy?"

I coughed. I used to think my mother didn't understand euphemism. I'd told her before that her bluntness, though never ill-intentioned, came off as rude. "You think the truth cares about being liked?" she had argued. After that I knew it was useless to try and soften her.

"Yes, Mom, a white boy."

"Be careful with those." She was carrying the Crock-Pot to the table. I slid my phone into my pocket. "He's just a friend."

The pot hit the placemat with a soft thud. Head down, my mother picked up her pace. She took the remaining spoon out of my hand and placed it in the empty bowl, adjusted the chopsticks so they were equidistant from their plates. I wanted her to challenge me, to voice her disbelief or, at the very least, her skepticism, but she wouldn't give me the pleasure. I was getting ready to lie again—"He's the new treasurer of senior council" or some other meaningless jargon—when she lifted the lid and steam ascended, the vapors at the top disappearing along with my resolve to push the matter further.

My belief is that she knew I was lying. I didn't have many friends in high school. Besides Ethan, Natalie was the only person I ever talked about or brought to the house, so my mom must have had some inclination that this white boy was more significant than I was letting on. But she was the type to bury her intuition, busy herself with the task at hand, make people think she was oblivious, lackadaisical, even, when really she was the keenest observer. She'd lost friends over fleeting remarks about someone's hair, another's spending habits. Her words were accusatory, and hurtful, but rarely false.

My mother's refusal of anything but the truth extended even into the imagination, so that for her, dreams were their own ugly little lies, as harmful as the ones that came out of our mouths. If life had made her this way, then by the time she had me it had become genetic, a Lamarckian feat. In lieu of dreams she and I had expectations, and to us the two couldn't be more different. Expectations you could work toward, be held accountable for. Dreams, on the other hand, existed in that realm of possibility in which there were variables beyond our control. Expectations demanded honesty. Dreams, deception.

Because of this I never pursued painting as anything more than a hobby. I'd entertained the idea of going to art school, telling my father I'd go if I got into Parsons. Then, midway through junior year, I decided not to apply.

"You could be the next Picasso," my dad said. "Ever think about that?"

"You don't even like Picasso," I replied.

"He's the most famous and most prolific artist."

I told him I didn't want to devote my life to something people would only appreciate after I was dead. "Besides," I added, "No one is sitting in a Salon, trying to have a discussion about culture and the human condition. These days everyone is too busy fucking bitches and getting money."

Hard lines appeared on my father's face, etching a pained expression. "What?" he said.

"Nothing."

I was feeling unfocused, in a fugue. The SATs were in a

week, and the capricious November weather had left me with a bad cold. I blew my nose into a tissue and said, "It's a line from a rap song."

That week had passed with feverish haste. I remember flipping through flash cards and balancing equations, but I couldn't tell you which vocabulary words gave me the most trouble—*torpor*? *ostensible*?—and I can still picture the circles and dotted lines, but it's been so long since I've thought about slope and intercept, sine and cosine, that now these images contain no meaning.

I recall my mother not sleeping. She did laps around the house, rearranging couch pillows, scrubbing the stovetop, peeling grapefruits—the outer layer first and then the membrane—until one or two in the morning.

"Go to sleep," I said to her every night. "You're not helping."

She would nod impatiently as she set down a plate of artfully arranged grapefruit, pushing aside papers and books to make room.

We met up the next day at a coffee shop in Montrose. I kept forgetting his name and would stay silent while I tried to remember it. These stretches went unnoticed because Collin had a lot of theories about the universe, dogs, retail, aerobic exercise.... By the time his name came back to me, the conversation had derailed so far from what it was about a minute ago that I had no idea what or how to contribute.

Eventually I stopped trying. Collin was perfectly content talking to himself. It reminded me of something my mother had told me years ago: Men aren't looking for women to talk to, they're looking for women who are pretty and will listen. Thirteen then, I wasn't sure if it was a lesson on the virtue of female docility or a warning against the vices of men. Now I still wasn't sure, but it no longer mattered. I began viewing what she said as evidence, proof that my mother had a past and that men who weren't my father were part of it.

"I've started meditating lately." I had wandered off again.

"What I've come to understand is that everything is temporary."

He said it like it was a novel idea, like he was on the brink of something. I scrambled to put it in context.

"We're all going to die, and really, every fear we have, no matter how big or small, is a fear of death."

I tried to wring meaning out of the vagueness. "True," I said.

He blew out his cheeks and fell back in his chair. "Want to head out?" he said. "We can pick up some beers and chill at my place. My roommate's out of town."

At the mall, I'd assumed he was my age, an upperclassman at one of the various surrounding high schools. It was his face that had thrown me off. Clean-shaven and paler than the rest of him, a cherubic roundness with pink cheeks to match. The pimples along his jaw were like coordinates on a graph. I had the urge to put a ruler to his skin and draw a best-fit line.

There must have been some reaction on my face. "How old are you again?" he asked me.

"Twenty-one," I lied, then wished I'd said twenty or twenty-two. My answer felt too precise. "You?"

"I'm old," he said. "Twenty-three. You in school?"

I told him I was taking some time off to figure out what I wanted to do. He said that was smart, and then went off about the societal pressures that make you feel like you *have* to go to college when really, you don't. You could enter the real world right out of high school and be just fine.

The beer tasted like Chinese medicine, bitter, so I drank it fast. He offered another and I said no thanks. I wanted to stay sober. I felt like it wouldn't count otherwise.

While Collin set up the TV, my thoughts settled onto Ethan, who'd become, in my mind, a deflated version of himself, all qualities sucked away, leaving behind only the distorted skin. We'd been together since freshman year but had known each other since we were twelve. At a neighorhood potluck where we met, he pushed me on a trampoline and was forced by his mother to apologize. I had cried on the spot, not out of pain or because I fell, but from the shock of another person's hands on me. Even then I knew I liked him.

On Saturday afternoons his parents taught Chinese School in an old church across town, and for those four hours we were alone. The box of condoms we bought together was probably still under his bed. I wondered if it had been opened.

Every time we were fooling around, my mother's apparition would appear. I would open my eyes as Ethan's hand slipped over me and there she'd be, standing next to his dresser, her glare neither approving nor disapproving, just a severe blankness.

Not altogether different from how she looked when, in December, I told her that he and I were broken up.

She had said calmly, dismissively, "He can't break up with you," followed quickly by, "Not without a good reason."

We were in front of the mirror in my room. I was dabbing concealer around my eyes. "I only told you because I didn't want you to hear it from his mom." Our families had grown close through us. "Now that you know, feel free to bring it up with her."

"What did he say was his reason?"

I tossed the makeup sponge and shrugged. "He said he doesn't want to go to college with commitments."

"That's all he said? What does that mean?" She leaned against the doorframe and folded her arms over her stomach, hands cradling sharp elbows.

I grabbed my backpack off the bed and imagined my mother falling off a bridge. "Do I have to spell things out for you?"

"Yes," she said. "Spell it out. Did something happen?"

"Why don't you ask his mom."

"I'm asking you."

I threw my bag over my shoulder. "You're annoying me," I said. "You're being vexatious. I'm going to be late for school."

It was a trick I had learned. My mother was afraid of English words she didn't know.

She stared at me like I was an everyday object slightly off-kilter. A slanted telephone pole. A chipped mug.

Collin made popcorn and put on a sci-fi movie. I hated sci-fi, and apparently he wasn't a big fan either. He fell asleep in the first ten minutes.

I checked my phone for texts and missed calls. I'd told my mom I would be at Natalie's working on a biology project and that I wouldn't be home until midnight or later. Still, it was 11 P.M. on a Sunday. I had school tomorrow. I was surprised she didn't want to make sure I was where I said I'd be, doing what I said I'd be doing.

Recently she'd been acting unlike herself. Twice in the last week, we'd eaten dinner late because she forgot to start the rice cooker. Before that, my dad came home to an unmade bed and panicked, thinking someone had broken in; my mother hadn't left a bed unmade since before they were married. She had started humming Chinese folk songs to herself with an expressiveness I'd never heard from her before.

"Your mother used to sing like this all the time," my dad said. We were taking a break from our books to watch her pin damp shirts onto a clothesline in the backyard. She had made the line herself, fixing a rope from one tree to another. "She's singing 'Jasmine Flower' now. It's a famous song. Everyone in China knows it."

Without any announcement, a relaxed atmosphere settled in our home. Books lay splayed on armrests, revealing where I and my father had been, and my mother, whom I'd never known to tolerate a mess, no matter how small, would walk right past. She no longer pestered us about separating our socks from our underwear in the wash or got upset when we used the counter rag to do the floor rag's job and vice versa. She left dirty dishes in the sink overnight.

"To soak," she said, which was the excuse I liked to use.

I asked my father if he thought her behavior was odd.

"Your mother's just happy that you've committed to a good school," he said. "She knows how hard you've worked."

I thought my dad was stupid at first, to be so clueless. But then I found it admirable. My father loved my mother, which made it only a little sad that he might never understand her.

An explosion in the movie jolted Collin awake. His head lurched forward. He ran his hands through his hair as he leaned slowly into the couch again.

"How long was I out for?" he asked. "What's happening in the movie now?"

On the screen, two men wearing masks were crouched behind a pillar holding guns.

"I think that guy from the beginning got shot," I said.

He came back from the kitchen with two bottled waters. "It's too bad I missed that."

We drank our waters while his eyes stayed on the TV. I checked my phone again. "Your boyfriend message you?" Collin set his half-empty bottle on the coffee table next to mine.

I looked up and gave him a pursed, tight-lipped smile. "Don't have one of those."

And then, in what my mother would have called an exercise in propriety, I did what I figured was the only correct thing to do in the situation. I swept my hair behind my neck and swung my leg around. Straddled on top of him, I put my hands around his neck and pulled myself closer.

We started kissing. Our rhythms were off. He liked to use

tongue and I didn't, but I was able to adjust, wiggling my tongue in his mouth in a way that I thought he might like. We moved to the bedroom. He bit my neck and touched me in places I felt most self-conscious about: my fleshy hips, my flat chest.

After things ended with Ethan, I lost my appetite. I lost twelve pounds in a month. My head had started looking disproportionately large. My hair became thin, fraying at the ends, and began falling out.

"Jia, you have to eat," my mother said, standing over my bed with a bowl of tofu seaweed soup, my favorite, only for me to coil into a fetal position and face the other way.

Despite her assurances that I looked the same as before, I still thought the weight had redistributed funny. My appetite returned eventually, ravenously, and I regained all of what I had lost but to different places. As Collin ran his hands along my body, I felt like I was the one roaming a new landscape, exploring its textures, dips, and folds.

I was afraid it would be painful. As my underwear brushed against my legs, stopping at my ankles in a tangle of lace, I thought, *I don't have to.* But as he fumbled with the condom, his very pink penis erect and resolute, I got scared of what would happen if I tried to back out now.

I scanned the room for my mother, expecting to meet her harsh, indifferent stare. I didn't find her.

During it I kept forgetting his name. It wouldn't stick for some reason. He was on top of me the whole time. Whenever he tried changing positions, I wrapped my legs tighter around his waist. Afterward I checked for blood.

He crawled into bed next to me wearing just his boxers. "That was great," he said.

The only liquid I saw was clear, spotting the white bed sheet gray. The sex had not been enjoyable, but it also hadn't hurt at all. I was still a little wet.

His name came back to me. Collin. *Col-lin*. "I actually have to go," I said to him.

"Why? You're welcome to stay."

He was making the decision for me, pulling the covers over my naked body and putting his heavy arm around my shoulder so that we lay spooning. Just as he started pressing his nose to the back of my neck, I heard my phone ring from the living room.

"I have to get that," I said, and before he could say anything, I threw the covers aside and ran to the couch, dancing over the cold tiles on the balls of my feet.

My phone was sliding off a white canvas pillow when I picked it up.

"Ma," I said, out of breath.

"What are you doing, running a marathon?"

My mother's voice gave me sudden clarity of my surroundings. Little details came into focus: the water rings on the coffee table, a California-shaped stain on the pillow where my phone had been sitting. Above the TV, held in place by thumbtacks, was a horizontal banner that I hadn't bothered to read until now: *PASSION IS ASCENSION*, in black italicized letters. DVDs were stacked on the windowsill. An orange paper lantern hung from the ceiling in the kitchen, the Chinese symbol for love painted on it.

A profound giddiness came over me as I soaked in the high-definition, inane ugliness.

"It's past midnight."

"We just wrapped up," I said. "I'm coming home." At that moment, the clarity turned inward, and I became acutely aware that I was speaking to my mother naked. "Why are you awake?" I asked.

"Bathroom," she replied. "You have your key?"

"I have it."

"Okay then. Good night, Jia."

Back in Collin's room, I dressed quietly. He was asleep in the other direction, as though he'd found someone else to spoon in my absence. I got as far as my right sock before he stirred and turned to face me.

"My mom wants me home," I said, twisting the sock so the heel pouch aligned properly.

He yawned and stretched his arm out behind him. "I get it." He folded a pillow in half and laid his head down. "Are you close with her?"

"Who?"

"Your mom."

"Not really," I said. "I just do whatever she says."

"Why?"

"I don't know." It came out sounding bitter, but I hadn't meant it to. I stood from the bed and tried to flatten the creases in my shirt.

"I think it's cool that you and your mom are tight like that," he said.

He'd misunderstood me, but he spoke with distinct tenderness, a note of longing. He was silly and ridiculous, the whole night had been silly and ridiculous, but he wasn't indecent. If I had asked him to stop earlier, I was pretty sure he would have.

"I'll text you in the morning?" he said mid-yawn.

"I look forward to it," I replied. I avoided looking at him as I walked out of his room into the living room to gather my things.

That night I walked up the driveway comforted by the sight of my house. It wasn't anything special, the one-story I'd grown up in, but the stillness of it behind the small movements of our oak tree, leaves and branches swaying to create shadows that danced on red brick, gave it an impressive, solid quality that made Collin's apartment seem imagined. It was already receding from my memory, like a place encountered in a dream.

All the lights were off inside. I left my sandals by the door and thought about wearing slippers. My mom didn't like when our feet tracked dirt into our carpeted rooms, onto our beds, but the plastic shoes made a *pat-pit-pat* sound as they dragged across wood and I wasn't in the mood for noise.

I walked in the dark to the kitchen and opened the fridge.

"Hungry?"

Still holding the door open, I twisted around. "You startled me," I said to my mom.

"Sorry. Are you hungry?"

The fridge was packed. There were two plates of leftover dumplings sealed in Saran Wrap and a Tupperware filled with my dad's barbecued chicken legs. I could also make something. The fridge was freshly stocked with whole wheat and white bread, carrots, broccoli, tomatoes, shredded cheese, three kinds of mushrooms, tofu, green onion, sliced ham and turkey, eggs. But I really wasn't hungry. Sometimes I just liked knowing my options.

"No," I answered.

"Ethan called while you were out," my mother said. She opened the door to the backyard.

"What did he want?" I had blocked his number months ago. "Where are you going?"

"To sit for a while. I can't sleep."

She left the door open. The air was surprisingly dry by Houston's standards, and cool. We sat in lawn chairs. A breeze ran its fingers through the leaves on our pear and fig trees. The hairs around my mother's face went flying while the rest stayed confined in a clip.

"What did he want?" I asked again.

"He said he called you but the call wouldn't go through."

"Anything else?" I hugged my knees to my chest, sinking lower into the woven strips of plastic.

"He wants to talk and asked if I could tell you to call him back." She paused, then said with ease, "I told him to stop calling us."

I faced her, but she stayed looking forward. My mom didn't believe in sentimental moments. She preferred to let emotions slip away unidentified. I never would find out what Ethan's call was about. I was curious, but I couldn't backpedal on what my mother had said. I could hear the sternness in her voice when she spoke to Ethan on the phone, and it seemed right that she would be the one to end things. I'm sure Ethan felt the same way. He would never call again.

We listened to coyotes and dogs, their howls puncturing the night from various points in the distance. My mother shifted in her seat.

"Can I ask you something?"

I waited.

"Did you want to go to art school?"

I had thought she was going to ask about Ethan.

"No," I said. "I mean, not really, not seriously. There are other things I'd like to do more."

"Your dad thinks if I hadn't pressured you so much, then maybe you would have applied to Parsons."

I laughed too loud for this time of night. Birds shot out from a tree in our neighbor's yard. Their silhouettes cut across the full moon.

"What does Dad know?" I said.

The statement proved satisfactory. We leaned back in our chairs. A minute passed, followed by another. In our silence, the once serene chirping of crickets turned urgent and foreboding, tiny screams for help.

"In college," my mother said at last, "you will find a nice Chinese boy, one who will treat you right."

Just like that, we were talking about Ethan again.

"Why does he have to be Chinese?"

"Easier that way. Look, it's always been easy for me and your dad."

In the years that followed, revisiting this moment would become an obsession of mine. Whatever run-ins she'd had with danger, they had nothing to do with me. That was what I thought, and I would spend the better part of my young adulthood determining what was safe based on what I could get myself to do in spite of her, learning only much later that acting against someone was also a way of abiding them.

"Good for you guys," was all I said then.

She raised one knee and began massaging her bare foot. "Now that you're going to college, your father and I are thinking about moving back to China."

This news, though it couldn't have been prefaced worse, did not surprise me. I almost expected it at the same time that I could not have seen it coming.

"Don't worry," she said. "We'll visit you all the time, and you can visit us whenever you want."

"I'm not worried," I said.

"You have a bright future ahead of you, Jia. I'm proud."

She meant this, I could tell, but the timing of it felt like an affront.

"I didn't do it for you," I said.

She put her foot down and squinted at a far corner of the yard, as though she'd seen something. Then her eyes went back to normal.

"How was your evening?" she asked.

There was something in the way she said it—her tone: amused, condescending—that made me believe she knew. At school the next day, I would spill to Natalie the details of losing my virginity. I would tell her that my mom knew somehow, and Natalie would say that as usual I was being paranoid. And yet, sitting next to her outside, both of us waiting on fatigue, I couldn't shake the feeling that my mother had been there the whole time, in that room in that ugly apartment with that ordinary man, hidden so I couldn't find her.

Silence

Since arriving unexpectedly three days ago Hui had spent most of her time in her room, and Meng did not ask what was wrong or try to get her granddaughter out of bed. Hui's father had mentioned heartbreak over the phone.

Meng had not asked for more details. That was what Hui liked about her grandmother, that she did not assume intimacy with anyone. Her mother had called her grandmother cold following the divorce from Hui's father, declaring that she was glad for the severed connection. Hui was fourteen at the time and had sensed that her mother's scorn was imprecise and therefore less worthy of respect. She'd felt similarly this summer whenever her mother recited embarrassing clichés, like "Different flowers match different eyes," that were meant to be comforting.

When Hui was in middle school, her father started an affair with the downstairs neighbor, a plain-looking woman who for years had given Hui candy in the evenings when she came home from school. Hui had wondered, after her father remarried to the woman, whether the candies were innocent or part of what had been taking place illicitly, but by then she had seen what could happen if one didn't hold one's hatred steady. Only a year after the divorce,

Hui's mother fell out with nearly all her friends, stating that one was too needy, another not attentive enough. She picked up the habit of badgering service people, and eventually her contempt encompassed her daughter too, and she would shame Hui about her weight and the acne that sometimes puffed up her face, telling her she ate too much junk food and spent too much time in places where the air was dirty. Hui did not wish to become like her mother, so she was determined to be pleasant to her father's wife, her stepmother, on the occasions when they had to interact. Meanwhile she regarded her father with calculated distance, responding to him out of necessity while hardly meeting his eyes.

Her father still lived in Xi'an, though no longer in the apartment where the affair had taken place. Meng was impressed by Hui's determination to keep her father accountable in ways that were fresh. She had chosen a random American school for college despite getting into one of the best universities in Shanghai. Just last New Year, she announced she was changing majors from chemistry to business because it was the easiest way for her to support herself and her mother out of college. What could Shujie say? He was a language professor and looked down on business as the kind of path someone pursued only when they had no real talents to offer, but he was the one who'd left Hui in her situation.

When Shujie's daughter from his second wife turned three last year, it was Hui who threw her half sister a birthday party. At the party, which Meng attended sitting quietly off to the side, Hui baked a cake and curled ribbons on pink balloons, playing host to everyone except her father, making him appear as a straggler in his own home. For most of the party, he'd stood with his hands behind his back, staring out the window at the street. Xinxin, whose birthday it was, had cried "Jiejie, don't go!" when she saw her big sister and grandmother putting their shoes on at the end of the night.

Hui owned a key to Meng's apartment. Meng had given it to her when she was fourteen, a day before she moved to Shanghai with her mother once it had become clear that the marriage was over. Meng had predicted her granddaughter's life becoming more complicated following the divorce, but she couldn't have guessed that year after year, Hui would continue refusing to sleep under the same roof as her father, using Meng's place as another instance of remaining close yet just out of reach. "She will still see me, at least," Shujie had said many times, consoling himself. Meng thought it would be a kindness if she just cut him off but did not say this out loud.

She set two bowls of rice porridge on the table and walked back to the kitchen for jars of pickled vegetables. When she returned, Hui was sitting cross-legged on a chair, turning the porridge over with a spoon. Her hair was greasy; her face was still bloated from sleep. Meng anticipated another quiet morning, each passing the time in a chamber of her own thoughts.

"Nainai, have you ever been in love?" Hui asked, staring intensely at the steam rising from her bowl.

They sat there, taking each other in through veils of steam. Meng had gotten used to fielding questions over the years, having lived unconventionally for a woman of her generation. It was always the same question in different disguises: Had her husband stepped out? Did he travel a lot for work? Remarking at a dress she tried on at a store once, a long time ago, a saleslady, seeing Meng's teenage son, said it was in the style that her husband would appreciate.

"I don't have a husband," Meng always answered, looking the person straight on and watching as they fumbled with what to say next.

Hui's question was without pretense. Now she was the one fumbling.

"No," Meng replied, scooting into the table.

"What about with Yeye?"

The idea of being in love with her ex-husband, from whom she'd been separated more than thirty years, almost made Meng laugh.

"No," she said.

"Why did you marry him, then?"

Hui noted the smooth pouches of flesh around her grandmother's eyes and tried to picture what she must have looked like when she was young, but her grandmother had a set quality about her, her expressions being limited and therefore hard to read, as though she had learned to keep herself within certain parameters. Since Hui was born Meng had been by herself, yet Hui had never thought to ask about it until now. Meng knew that one's interest in others is a door that is opened by one's own suffering.

Where to begin? Every story relied on one preceding it, which made a story told in isolation a lie and one told in its entirety basically impossible. At the time when she'd asked her husband for a divorce, the major events in her life had already passed. It was the common everyday grievances that disturbed her. Her husband wasn't a bad person, she told Hui, but he was useless in all practical matters. The thought of asking him one more time to pick up flour at the end of the month or to stop by the pharmacy on his way home for Shujie's allergy medication, tasks he could never remember to do on his own, became to her the greatest confirmation of life's futility, greater than innocent people being killed or her own father's untimely death. Quanli didn't drink or gamble or hold grudges against other men. Through his party connections Meng secured a job as a bank teller, a lifelong government position that could be passed down and that came with a good pension. Even her friends thought she was crazy to ask for a divorce and cruel to carry the marriage on in silence.

"As long as he refused the paperwork, I refused to speak to him. It went on like this for two years, us not speaking, until a buddy of his paid me a visit while your grandfather was out."

Meng gestured at the apartment that she and Hui were in now. The visit must have occurred in June. That was the time every year when she made zongzi, packing rice into bamboo leaves that she fashioned in the palm of her hand. She was focused severely on the task that day, wrapping one zongzi and then another while the friend pleaded with her.

"Forgive him for whatever he's done, the friend kept saying," Meng said to Hui. "There's no sense in a life like this, dwelling together and never speaking."

"There is no sense in a lot of what we do, I wanted to reply. I didn't think our situation was so far-fetched."

"I don't know," said Hui. "Two years is a pretty long time to not talk to somebody. A pretty long time to be ignored."

"I advised the friend his energy would be better spent finding my husband a new woman to marry," Meng said, "instead of trying to convince me to change my mind. You're right. Two years was more than enough time. My husband should have a companion. We should both live happily."

Hui was surprised her grandmother was telling her all of this. What her mother called cold Hui had always interpreted as her grandmother's passivity, an impressive lack of desire for control. As far back as she could remember, her Nainai had neither doted on her nor reprimanded her, not even when she was a small child, begging for a light-up toy being sold on the street or running headlong into gray puddles after it rained, ruining her pretty dresses.

"You would return from your Nainai's looking ragged," her mother liked to say, after she had written the old woman off. "That woman couldn't have cared less."

But Hui saw how her grandmother tended to the plants in

her sunroom, visiting them at the same hour every day to adjust their placement under the light; how she had given Hui the key to her apartment when she was fourteen without offering any advice, not even "I'm sorry" or "Good luck," the key being the only useful acknowledgment of Hui's helplessness that she'd received, proving to her that her grandmother was not careless; she simply moved in such a way as to conserve energy. That Meng was sharing so much now made Hui nervous. She felt she should share something in return.

"Your food is getting cold," Meng said, noticing Hui's expression turn dour where it had been bright and inquisitive just a moment ago. She was still hunched over her porridge, even though it had stopped steaming. The top layer was beginning to congeal.

"We both got what we wanted ultimately," Meng continued, thinking that for Hui's sake she should try to provide a satisfying story ending. "I even attended your grandfather's wedding."

It had been his one condition, Meng explained, that she be there as a way of publicly giving her blessing. Otherwise people would think him imprudent for marrying again so quickly. They had agreed to this, and to the divorce, in the first conversation they had in two years, the last one they ever had.

"Sounds awkward," Hui said, relieved that her grandmother had more to say. "Was my Ba there? At the wedding?"

"Your father was there, yes," Meng replied, thinking back to the small banquet hall that had since been converted to a karaoke bar. She was heartened that Hui was imagining Shujie in this context. They had been around the same age when their families fell apart, and while the circumstances were different, where there was sympathy, Meng thought, it was always possible to find some connection.

"He deserted me the moment we entered the venue and sat with his uncles at the table closest to the bride and groom, while

I sat in the back by the swinging doors where servers rushed in and out.

"It was me and the bride's distant relatives at my table. One very old lady, blind and nearly deaf, asked what relation I had to the new couple, and I told her I was an old friend. She nodded and didn't ask more questions.

"Our friends and acquaintances, the people to whom my presence meant something, saw me and either looked too long or avoided eye contact. I didn't want to be there, but it wasn't more awkward than my own wedding when I was nineteen, after having met your Yeye only once. At least the second time he got married, the two of us were no longer strangers."

Hui uncrossed her legs and leaned forward, setting her elbows on the table. "It sounds like you two were not compatible," she said, looking pleased with herself for casting an easy judgment.

Compatibility took on many forms, Meng wanted to say, but she'd heard the term a lot lately on dating talk shows and decided to spare herself the likelihood of being misunderstood. When she and Quanli met, she'd pitied his bad teeth, brown in the crevices from malnutrition, a feeling that she mistook for affection. He'd grown up in poverty to become a high-ranking official in the army. By the time they got together, Meng had been labeled in their village as the daughter of Lipeng, a former landlord. Their match was viewed as complementary, their marriage as politically sound.

Modern-day compatibility had more to do with personality and taste. People seemed to be searching for themselves in others as opposed to a person who could make up their shortcomings.

"You could have found someone else afterward, like Yeye did," Hui said when Meng didn't respond. "That could have been your chance."

"My chance?"

"At finding romance."

This display of hopefulness made Meng blush. She was relieved to see that whatever damage had been done to Hui, it was not irrevocable. At the same time, she thought if it was romance that her granddaughter was seeking, she would have no trouble finding it, but whether it came with love would be a separate question.

"Your father was innocent when all of this happened," Meng said, trying to direct the discussion away from herself. "It's natural for children to want to see their parents together. He stayed angry with me for a long time."

"You weren't a coward at least. You were honest with your family." Hui sighed, then laughed unevenly.

"My father's a hypocrite."

Meng had only said what was on her mind, but Hui had taken that for the answer to her question.

"My remaining alone had nothing to do with your father's feelings," Meng clarified. "I'd grown tired of company. That's all."

She refrained from delving into it further, it seeming needless to say certain things to her granddaughter when at more critical points in her life she'd chosen silence as a measure of inflicting her will. There were many people who deserved her apology, and she'd apologized to none of them, out of both pride and shame. Sometimes the only way to redeem one's actions was to abide by them. In those final, quiet two years of their marriage, she and Quanli had moved around each other, repeating the same motions every day from different angles, like line dancing. There was something she'd begun to miss about that only very recently, not Quanli exactly but also not *not* him, the hush of another's presence that fell like a spell upon any hour, making it go by faster. When Shujie left for college the silence took full effect, threatening to grow loud unless she kept herself constantly busy. She'd been foolish to think she could have solitude and at the same time avoid loneliness.

Hui was reclining, drumming her fingers on her stomach. There was color in her face now, now that her thoughts had found a target in her father. Anger was a livelier emotion than sadness.

Meng got up to reheat their food.

"Don't bother," said Hui. "I'm not hungry."

"You're graduating soon," said Meng. She wasn't used to talking this much and was worried she wouldn't be able to stop. "Are you looking forward to senior year?"

"Not really," said Hui, who guessed that her grandmother was changing the subject to distract her from thoughts of her father, or to gesture at the more recent heartbreak, but she refused to let one emotional obsession vilipend another; she resolved to contain them all and be equally unforgiving. Meng began clearing the table, putting the pickle jars back in the pantry, the bowls next to the sink. She came back to the living room with snacks that she kept around for whenever Xinxin visited, individually packaged strips of tofu and seaweed-flavored crackers, bags of chips, fruit leathers.

Hui tore into the crackers first, peeling back the bright yellow paper. "My ma would kill me if she saw me eating any of this."

"How is she doing?"

Meng lowered herself back into her seat.

"Fine, I guess."

Hui rested a cracker on her tongue and waited for the surface to just stick before taking the whole thing in her mouth.

Her mother was not fine, but the scale of that against Hui's own well-being was beginning to shift. Seven years after the divorce, Hui's mother still referred to her ex-husband's wife as his mistress and would try to pry details from Hui about her father's life, just so she could have reason to act more erratically. Last semester, she'd called in the middle of the night more than once, not minding the time difference, to show Hui a new painting or cross-stitch. She sent clickbait articles about women falling into the hands of adulterous men or men being lured to ruin by promiscuous women.

"Be careful," the accompanying message always read. It was depressing, viewing the world through her eyes.

She'd been nicer to Hui this summer, because she believed she and her daughter shared something now, now that they'd both been hurt by love. Hui did not like what that implied for her future.

"Your father is sorry over what happened."

Meng seized her desire to say this before it went away.

"It doesn't have to happen in one day, but you should start trying to let him back into your life. At least let him tell you he's sorry."

"I come home every holiday, don't I?" Hui replied with her mouth full. "What do you think that is?"

A way of making your absence pronounced, Meng thought. She gathered crumbs from the table into her hand.

"Don't be like me," she said, brushing the crumbs onto a napkin. "I pushed people away."

"Who else besides Yeye?"

When Meng was a teenager, she cut off all communication with her own father while the two still lived together. If Hui knew this about her grandmother, she might find that they had much in common, but revealing it would lead to other parts of the past that Meng wasn't prepared to talk about. The father she'd condemned as a capitalist died in a bike accident shortly after she got married. They hadn't started talking again before she buried him.

Their first argument had been over a rally taking place in the village square. He'd raised his voice at her, telling her he'd seen enough new leaders in his lifetime to know there would always be one more promising something different, dangling people's futures in front of them like a bone tied to a dog's back, sending them chasing after something that was never attainable. Meng was fifteen years old. In the square, she sat with other young people in wheelbarrows and on top of haystacks, smiling, cheering, waving flags as red streamers fell from the sky, Mao's words blasting through the loudspeakers.

She smashed relics around town and threw sand in her teachers' faces. What she and her comrades started ended up killing those kids in Beijing. Excitement and tragedy. What else was romance made of?

Hui was still in the phase of cherishing the worst of what had happened to her, but she would wake up one day and discover that the happiest memories were the most painful. Meng was six when she started walking to school accompanied by her father's voice. He would call to her across the barren back part of the village, where sheep went to graze and crops grew in scattered patches, most of the land too rugged to till, keeping her company as she made it past one landmark and then another. The nearest school was over a mile away. She picked up her knees and kept both hands out in front of her as she felt her way through the darkness.

"Mengmeng, have you reached the second bend!" he shouted.

"Going around it now!" she yelled back.

"Watch your step!"

Their voices echoed, as though multiples of them were spread out on every crest and crag.

Before descending the final peak that led into town, Meng looked back. By then, night would have peeled away just enough for her to make out her father, standing at the foot of the carved-out hill they called home. The meager light cast the world into depth. Hilltops emerged out of shadow.

"Study hard, Mengmeng!"

"Bye, Baba!" Meng shouted back, waving with such force that her heels rose off the ground.

She had to try to recall such details now. Most of the time when she remembered the past, everything struck her at once as a feeling.

"Are you okay, Nainai?"

Meng looked at Hui.

"What were you thinking about just now?"

"Nothing," she said. The feeling vanished.

"I need to get out of the house." Hui pushed her chair back. "I'm going for a walk."

"You haven't had a real meal. Let me pack you something."

"No thanks, Nainai," Hui called from her room. She emerged with her cell phone and purse. "I'll be back soon."

Prancing down the building's stairs, Hui concentrated again on the boy who had stopped returning her calls. Acknowledging another's pain obscured one's own. Hui wasn't ready yet to accept that. From the window, Meng watched her granddaughter walk up the tree-lined street. The old woman's longing was like that of a child, featuring prominently in her eyes, which captured that spirit from her youth. It would have been easy for anyone to picture what she had looked like back then, if anyone had been there.

One Day

On a random weekday in November, when I was a child and not yet weary of his kindness, my father drove forty minutes from his workplace to have lunch with me in the school cafeteria.

Handprint turkeys lined the halls of the school's first floor, from the entrance up to the library, then splitting in two directions down the various homerooms of K through third. Each little turkey was cut from a paper plate. Each colored brown in the palm, the turkey's chest, with a flash of red below the beak, the part we called the turkey's gobble. In the center we'd written our names. Eric, James, Annabelle…

"Helen," my father read out loud when he found mine.

He touched the fingers, which I'd decorated in orange and brown feathers and nothing else. The other turkeys were more exciting. Feathers in pink and blue and purple, plus glitter and sequins, pom-poms with bits of tinsel—but mine was the most realistic, I thought. During the craft, it had bothered me that no one else seemed to care about this. "Use your imagination, Helen!" Ms. Evans had said, but my imagination, I wanted to tell her, had rules. Even in kindergarten, it seemed plain to me that certain things were not possible.

"It's super," my father said, looking down at me. He smiled and touched the back of my head. "Are you hungry?"

In the cafeteria I scanned the mayhem, all those bodies in one fluorescent gray room, until I caught Ms. Evans, her stubby fingers spread wide and waving at me as though her explosion of hair or outfit wouldn't have given her away. I didn't have friends. Ms. Evans was always making efforts to include me, fold me in with the other kids, but I took my cues from adults, the other teachers, and I maintained a separation between me and her. The cafeteria smelled as it always did, of something fried and something sour. My classmates with packed lunches were already seated with their sandwiches, their baggies of grapes and baby carrots. Everyone else was in line, where I would have been, too, sliding a tray of pizza with a side of mashed potatoes, if on that day my father had not come and surprised me.

At the far end of the table, where no one was sitting yet except for us, he removed two clear containers from his lunchbox, both pocked with moisture on the inside. He looked around, then raised his hand in the air as though he were one of us, a student. He winked at me, sitting across from him, and I tried to wink back.

Ms. Evans was down one table, monitoring a different homeroom. She saw my father and made like she was running. Her pants swished. Her enormous arms rolled from side to side.

"Yes, Mr. Chen?" she said, out of breath.

"Is there a microwave somewhere so I can heat up our food?"

"Sure, if you come with me I can take you to the teacher's lounge right down the—"

Just as she finished the last word, Ms. Evans threw her head back and sneezed, sending one of her silver hoop earrings slicing through the air to the ground near our feet. The noise was so loud, the convulsion of her body so huge and terrifying, that I ducked and covered my face. My father tapped my knee three times before I moved my elbows away, before Ms. Evans could notice.

"Bless you," he said, and reached under the table.

When he resurfaced a moment later, Ms. Evans was blinking rapidly with wide, open eyes, like she'd just appeared someplace new. She sniffed, and instead of taking the earring my father had retrieved, she cocked her head sideways to remove the other hoop from her other ear.

"These things never stay in," she said. She spoke as though forced into admission. "They're cheap."

"They look nice on you," said my father. After a pause he added, "Cheers," lifting the earring to my kindergarten teacher, the hoop held solidly, daintily, between his thumb and index finger, in the signature for *Okay!*

Ms. Evans gasped. She let the breath go in a soft, choppy laugh, exposing something fragile, and I got the sense that for Ms. Evans, life had turned one way, the wrong way, a long time ago and now could not find its way back.

"Cheers," she said.

They clinked hoops, making a dull, disappointing sound.

We ate noisily and with our heads down, chopsticks flicking, the way we ate at home. By then the lines had cleared and the tables were full. The boys sitting next to us stared, and I thought nothing of it. My world was still too small for me to feel ashamed.

"What you did earlier, Helen," my father began once we were finished. "It wasn't nice." He stacked the empty containers on top of each other and pushed them aside. "You could have hurt your teacher's feelings."

I said, "I know."

My father began peeling an orange and carved the fruit out in seconds, in one tremendous sweep of his thumb. He broke it in half and gave one to me.

I wonder if he suspected then that I was beginning to detect weakness and to feel repulsed by it. "Helen is such a sweet girl," my father was always telling everyone. Over the years it became clear to me that he'd interpreted my reclusiveness for loneliness, my brooding for sophistication, when actually I was, as a child, already sick of the world and hardening myself to it, so it could never do to me what it had done to Ms. Evans. What it had done to my father, who raised me on his own. I thought he was too good for the feckless types on whom his charms were most effective, until eventually I viewed him as one of them, someone who did not know how to make life easier.

I left home when I was eighteen and remained distant until he got sick. When I returned, I watched a man turn into a gnarled, hollowed body, as though someone had taken a spoon to his skin and scooped out the flesh, and I knew, before being told, that something so small and destroyed could not survive. I've learned to be softer now, but there remains a frayed thread of that part of me from before. At times I feel it writhing—in my intolerance for slowness, my impatience—even though now I'm someone's partner and a mother to two children. I was twenty-five when he died.

"Don't go," I said to him when lunch was over. We were standing near the school's entrance. All around us, kindergarteners were filing out of the cafeteria. First graders were making their way in, a scene repeating itself.

"Baba has to go back to work. I'll see you in a few hours at home."

"But I don't want to be here," I said. The idea of resuming an ordinary day filled me with dread. "I want you to be with me."

My father knelt down. He aligned my hand to his in a still high-five and said, "Look! My turkey's so much bigger than yours."

When I said nothing, he draped my arms over his shoulders. "You'll make friends, I promise you," he said. "It gets better."

He kissed me firmly on the forehead, and I watched him leave. There was a spring in his step, the gait of someone strong and healthy. Ms. Evans came and stood with me by the glass doors, and to my surprise she did not turn me away. It wouldn't occur to me until I was an adult that, probably, no one had ever raised a toast to Ms. Evans before, that my father was likely the first, perhaps the only. Before that I couldn't appreciate the perfect strangeness of their encounter. Together we watched him get into his car and drive. I stared out even after he was gone, until I felt ready, then Ms. Evans walked me back to class.

Julia

When she was twenty-two she used to spend what little money she could have saved on hardcover books, lattes, and croissants. She read in cafés alone and anonymous, with no reason except to offer the world a glimpse of her. Ten years later, she was leaving and decided to revisit all her old haunts, thinking she could pack up the years the way she had packed up her things: taking them out of context and rearranging them so they fit compactly together. Outside a smoothie shop, she recited her usual in her head. The owner was a Jamaican man; he smiled at her through the window, and she waved. It occurred to her that he had no idea she was saying goodbye.

This sentimentality, purposefully spurred, waned quickly, almost instantly. She'd moved so many times in New York, across different boroughs, that the effect of leaving had all but worn off, and although her nostalgia was premature, it was the only way she could ensure this chapter would close with a proper sense of what had taken place. Not paying attention, she almost knocked heads with two girls coming out of a bodega. They stumbled onto the street, all limbs and hair, grasping each other. They were young women, upon closer inspection. College-age, about. Esther remembered what that had been like.

"Whoops!" she chirped, before pulling back and saying sorry.

The taller one shot her friend a furtive look, then laughed in Esther's face. She hooked her elbow to her friend's arm, and the two of them skipped down the street. Their hair clipped after them.

There was something horrible and familiar about that tall one, Esther thought, not moving from where she was, the way she'd dragged her friend away firmly yet delicately, like how a princess might usher her favorite servant when there was something urgent and secret they needed to discuss. She hadn't gotten a good look at the friend, and now she wished she had. She peered down the street where they had turned, but they were gone.

Back in Texas, Esther had met Julia through Rooney, a mutual friend and Esther's first roommate. They had remained distant for all of freshman year. They grew close while Julia was subletting Rooney's room for the summer.

"I didn't think you had depth," Julia said to Esther one night while they were lying on the carpet in the living room, staring mindlessly at the ceiling. Their summer break was coming to an end. In a week, Rooney would return to campus and Julia would return to her dorm. They had just smoked some weed and torn through a family-size bag of tortilla chips, leaving shards at the very bottom.

"You smile a lot. I didn't think someone so cheerful could be smart."

Despite her nonchalance, it was not a topic that had been raised before. The kitchen light was on, but otherwise the living room was dark. The fibers of the carpet pricked the back of Esther's neck and shoulders. She squirmed to allay the itching.

"By that logic," she ventured, "I should have thought you were a genius."

"And I'm not?" said Julia.

Esther turned to face her, but Julia stayed looking up.

"I think I just thought you were a bitch."

Julia laughed. Her chest jumped. "Well I was wrong. You're funny."

"I could be funny and dumb," Esther offered.

It had been a habit of hers, softening her viewpoint with self-deprecation.

Julia said no and made a comment about humor and intelligence. After that, they fell asleep on the floor.

Back in her almost-empty apartment, Esther poured herself a drink. Eight years had passed since she'd last seen Julia, in which time Esther had built a life for herself out of the virtues that Julia had imparted. The last she'd heard from Julia, she was getting married. The invitation came four months after their disastrous time in New York, after which they'd stopped speaking. She had flipped the embossed card back and forth, looking for a scribbled apology, or a note. She checked the envelope as well and found nothing. *Julia & John invite you to their wedding* was all it said, along with a date and location. *Merriment to follow.* Appalled at first, Esther was then sad, then fuming. She'd cut the invitation to pieces using scissors; the paper was too strong to tear.

On the couch, she brought her whiskey to her lips before remembering to raise it to the light. It delighted her that the ice was chiseled and completely clear, not a streak of cloudiness. The ice clinked liltingly as she swirled the glass. Now she sipped, savoring the bitterness on her tongue followed by a cold sting in the sides of her mouth. She'd boiled the water first, then added it to the tray.

Fancy ice; overnight oats made with meticulous spoonfuls of nuts and berries, making her feel like she was some highly evolved squirrel. She'd come to appreciate these rituals, their patterning and repetition securing dependable results, adding predictability and assurance to her days. She could have her overnight oats anywhere, in Houston, where she was from, or in Nashville, where she was moving soon to oversee the ancillary paper products line for a small, vaguely Christian publisher. Not books, but book-adjacent, she'd told friends when they asked why she was leaving. Back to her Southern roots! she joked. Her friends with a sense of humor had all left in the years preceding. The ones who remained stared at her with long faces.

When they asked what she would miss most about New York, she said the ubiquity of art, how it could be found on the streets and in museums, in the people and the ways they chose to live. She knew this was the answer they were seeking, the one that assuaged the precarious matter of continuing in New York, which was brought into question every time another person chose to leave. Art was what she loved about the city, what everyone loved, but it wasn't what she would miss. She would miss the drugstores that punctuated every block, some of them converted from beautiful old buildings, giving them that stumbleupon quality she'd have to do without in a place like Nashville, where people drove cars and drugstores were treated more respectfully as destinations. After work, or before a night ended, the rows of products provided a sense of order, filled with latent possibility. The colors—condoms, toothpaste, Zyrtec, folic acid—were brighter, more abrasive under white overhead lights. She loved going in and discovering a need she hadn't known was there. It felt good going home not empty-handed.

After her father died, two years after she and Julia had fallen out, she would walk twice down every aisle, finding more and more things to buy. Her grief had made her angry. The intensity of the emotion brought Julia to mind with a searing vengeance, as though the reaction she should have had to their friendship ending had been delayed, or could only be expressed in light of another, more straightforward tragedy. She thought about it but in the end couldn't bring herself to call.

That was six years ago. When you want someone's pity, her mother used to say, that's when you've lost all self-respect. Her mother had hated being a widow and remarried shortly after burying Esther's father. Before Julia, Esther was like a baby bird displaced from her nest. This was how she'd thought of herself, going as far as to specify her plumage—dark purple, an attractive color that did not announce itself too loudly. Growing up, she chirped pleasantly, incessantly, at her peers, thinking that by appearing helpless she might earn people's trust. Julia was the one who'd scooped her up and taken her home, fed her nutrients through a dropper, so that by the time Esther's father died she was strong enough to fend for herself, even without Julia. She had kept her heartaches (there were two) private, giving herself permission to party and drink and work as much as she needed while discussing how she felt with no one, not even Bobby, who'd been her closest friend after Julia and the person she'd hurt the most by turning inwardly morose, outwardly exhaustive.

What was so bad about wanting to be pitied? She was reminded she owed her mother a call. Being adored—wasn't that basically the same thing?

That summer, they had stayed up late talking in Esther's room or Julia's, which was technically Rooney's room, a fact they frequently overlooked. Their similarities—like that they were both children of immigrants, Esther's parents Chinese, Julia's Bulgarian—were unspectacular, looking back, but had felt crucial in a phase when they were searching for themselves in others. Their black hair looked identical but turned different shades under the sun. They played word games. "What a good dog," one person would say. Then they took turns. "What a kind dog." "What a beneficent dog." And so on until they reached something absurd—"What a priestly dog!"

They'd keel over with laughter, in the grocery store, in the library's all-quiet section, reveling in dirty looks from strangers, even better if the looks came from people they knew. They'd both been the children of bad marriages.

"Cowards," Julia had said, about both sets of parents when it came up that neither could go through with divorce. "Adults are full of crap."

Before Julia, Esther never felt qualified to make judgments like these on her own.

Esther shared her loneliness as an only child.

"The fantasy of a companion became my companion," she tried to explain one afternoon. They were in Julia's room, again on the floor. There was a bed, Rooney's bed, and a nightstand on which they'd set their melting iced coffees. It was an old apartment building, poorly maintained, full of cracks and crevices where dirt could hide. The daylight illuminated small particles in the air. "I had a friend group in high school, but it always bothered me that they didn't like me for the same reasons I liked myself. When I was twelve, I had a miniature plastic rocking horse that I brought with me everywhere. I don't even remember how I got it, but I spoke to it in the shower and before bed and in the mornings after I just woke up. That's sort of how it feels now when I like someone." She meant *like someone* as in a crush. As in a boy. Boys were what they talked about when they weren't bringing up their childhoods. "I get obsessed. I imagine us being in constant communication and run the risk of feeling closer to them than they feel to me, but that doesn't even matter in the end, because it's the fantasy that sustains me."

Julia was listening.

"It's pathetic," Esther said, turning away. "I know."

"It's not."

Julia folded Esther's hand and placed it over her—Julia's—heart.

When the semester started, Rooney took her room back, but

they found it increasingly difficult to be apart and burdensome to be together when others were around, so in the spring they found their own apartment. A week before the move, Esther was in her room, eating grapes and typing a paper. Most of her things were in boxes. Rooney entered without knocking.

"You could have at least had a conversation with me," she said, her voice sounding tattered. "How do you think it makes me feel, being deserted in my own home? You're so exclusive when you're with her." She shifted her weight and ended up back in her original stance. "Always whispering and giggling about nothing."

Esther felt her nostrils tighten. She couldn't tell if she was embarrassed for herself or for Rooney, who was waving her heart like a flag in front of Esther's face. It was true they hadn't included Rooney in any of the recent changes. "What was that?" Rooney would ask whenever she caught on to one of their games. "Nothing nothing," came their reply, as they strained to look in opposite directions. When Julia slept over now, as a guest, it was always in Esther's bed. In the mornings they would walk to the Shipley's across the street and order a donut each plus a dozen holes to share. It never occurred to them to pick up something for Rooney.

"You know what Julia used to say about you? She said you seemed desperate, that people only like you because you reek of insecurity. I wasn't going to tell you, but it's like you've forgotten that I exist, you and her both. You're both cunts."

Rooney burst into tears. Esther's impulse was to get up and apologize, but instead she thought what Julia would do, and she sat there. She watched Rooney cry.

"It's not like you don't have other friends," she said, once Rooney was depleted to hiccups.

"Oh, fuck you," said Rooney, before turning and slamming the door.

On the itinerary for Sunday, Esther's last, was paying a visit to her very first apartment. She found a crumpled sundress in a box labeled Give Away. She put it on and noticed tiny fibers stuck to the cheap polyester. Last night, thoughts of Julia had kept her awake, threatening the cheerful accord she was determined to leave the city with, her time here like a stone she'd been polishing.

Getting off the bus, she felt self-conscious. There was some fear, an uncanniness, that the girls from yesterday were going to appear, Julia's young doppelgänger making fun of her about her dress that kept riding up at the waist and because what she was doing, her committed wistfulness to what she was doing, was a cliché. She knew it was, but so was coming here in one's twenties from whatever sad hometown one wished to escape. Everyone who left the city arrived at the same conclusion: the real alternative life was in the suburbs, where no one deluded themselves into believing a harder life was somehow more worthwhile. Esther smiled. She scooped her hair to one side of her neck, giving the other side to the breeze. Just those girls wait and see.

With graduation looming, they each applied for jobs in New York. It was Esther who got lucky, receiving an offer from an academic publishing house while Julia accepted a job nearby, thinking she would use it to build her résumé. For a while after Esther moved, they stayed talking every night.

"Can you imagine what it'll be like when we're both living there?" Julia said on the phone. From the sound of her voice, Esther could tell she was lying on her stomach.

Julia was a lab tech at a small private university not far from where they'd gone to school. The pay was low, lower than what Esther expected for someone who'd double majored in science, and the work was lonesome, Julia had mentioned more than once. She had only one coworker. But this was only temporary, they both believed. There was a life together waiting for them.

"You'll be doing research at Columbia or NYU," Esther said. "I'll be editing books at one of the big trade houses. We'll grab bagels, walk around Central Park."

Julia squealed, even though neither of them liked bagels that much, and it turned out Central Park was much harder to get to than a drugstore, especially when home was in an outer borough.

One Sunday, Julia called in the middle of the night, crying. Esther asked what was wrong and felt uplifted to be the one asking.

The guy Julia had been seeing had just broken up with her in an email.

"I'm particular, he wrote," said Julia, still catching her breath. "I rearranged the furniture in his house, which apparently upset him, though he never told me. I never would have done that if I had known."

"You wouldn't have?" Esther asked.

"No," said Julia.

"What setup did he have before?"

"That doesn't matter."

"I think it matters if you made an improvement."

"It doesn't matter!" Julia snapped. "Stop trying to prove how clever you are! It's not going to bring my relationship back!"

"Sorry," Julia said, when Esther was silent. "I don't mean to yell." She spoke softer now but still with an edge. "I'm heartbroken and not myself. Or maybe I'm exactly myself. Maybe that's why Steven dumped me. Because I'm a total bitch."

She spoke as though testing the statement out, or to see what Esther would say. But Julia *was* a bitch, and so was Esther. Since when had they cared? A minute passed, until she felt she'd missed her chance to say "No, no, of course not." Then Julia hung up.

It had started to rain. Esther considered buying an umbrella but was enjoying the sporadic drops on her head and arms, like tiny reassuring pats. She walked down a street of warehouses and storage facilities, turning left at a park on Bedford. The apartment was only a few blocks away, according to her phone GPS, but she couldn't tell if the setting was familiar. The flowering pear trees had shed their petals so that from a distance, it was as though the sidewalk were coated in a fine white powder. The wet petals gave off a sweet then rancid scent as Esther stepped on them.

A car sped past. She kicked a pebble onto the road. The wedding invitation had seemed like a jab in true Julia fashion, sharp and sly—*Merriment to follow*—but what if Esther had been wrong? What if the invitation *was* the apology? Then she'd rejected it. Even now, when someone, usually another woman, told Esther she was funny or intimidating, or mean, she knew it was Julia they were talking about, Julia they respected and feared. It always made her proud. She nearly tripped over a gap in the pavement.

Esther had just been promoted to associate editor when Julia visited. While her day-to-day was still mostly the same— scheduling, paperwork—she made slightly more money than before, as far as publishing salaries were concerned. Through Bobby, the boy she was seeing casually, she found freelance gigs writing music reviews, which got her free tickets to festivals and shows. Esther named these accomplishments and others as they climbed the bright spiraling halls of the Guggenheim.

Julia only nodded or said, "Nice." She didn't seem interested in the art either, shifting quickly from one painting to the next, the way one looks at cars for sale on the side of the road—curious one moment, the next moment totally out of mind. On the ferry to the Statue of Liberty, the first and last time Esther would make the trip, she asked about John, Julia's then new boyfriend. Julia gave mostly one-word answers.

"Good."

"Fine."

"Nice."

It felt like making small talk. Esther rambled on, annoying herself, dredging up old memories in the likelihood that something would stir Julia to engage.

There was a game they had played in college, called Alcoholic or Hemingway. Julia had invented it, a way of dividing boys into two groups, the posers and the intellectuals.

In front of a Chagall, Julia shook her head.

"Why did we play that game?"

"What do you mean why?"

"I mean what was it about?"

The game was about who was worthy of their attention and who wasn't. Esther said as much to Julia in those words, not really believing that she'd forgotten.

"Why were we so judgmental? What right did we have? If the genders were reversed, that game would be offensive," said Julia. "We'd be dicks if anyone ever found out."

Technically, they would be misogynists, but the genders weren't reversed. The parity was the point, she had thought. She asked Julia if everything was okay.

There was something robotic in the way Julia turned to face her, her eyes and her head moving along one axis.

"What, because I'm not in the mood to reminisce?"

Julia ascended the staircase, but Esther stayed looking at another painting. She'd assumed it was another Chagall based on the primary colors, but it turned out to be the work of another artist entirely.

The next day, she decided to match Julia's sullenness, thinking that doing so would wear Julia to her senses. They couldn't both suffer the silent treatment. Then on the Brooklyn Bridge, Julia told Esther she quit her job, and Esther asked why but was too relieved in the moment to care. Julia had been keeping a secret. Now it was out.

"I'm taking coding classes and waiting tables in the interim."

"But you love chemistry," said Esther. "That's your passion."

"Yeah, well, being a scientist is cute, but it's not going to pay the bills."

Julia stared out at the East River. She tucked some hair behind her ear, uselessly; the wind just tossed it up again.

"I'm surrounded by well-off people. John's an attorney. John's friends are attorneys."

"Everyone in Texas can't be an attorney."

"They've bought houses," said Julia. "They vacation to nice places."

"So? They're older than us."

"How old do you think they are? How young do you think we are?"

John was twenty-eight. They were twenty-four. Behind them a bike bell rang, and someone yelled, "Shit motherfucker!" Diamond flecks sprang off the water's surface.

"So they drown in legalese most of their lives so they can take a trip to Tulum every few months. Who cares?"

Julia straightened, and Esther braced herself. Then Julia said, "Can't you just be happy for me?"

"Jules. I'm sorry. I am." She was. "I just don't think it's useful to make comparisons, that's all. You're not inferior to those people."

"People like my boyfriend."

Esther was having trouble finding the right footing for the point she was trying to make.

"Yes, like John. There's nothing wrong with him or his friends, but there's nothing wrong with you or me either. We have our ambitions. We're just starting out. We still have so much time."

Julia's hair was everywhere, licking her face, her shoulders, while the rest of her remained motionless.

"It's called computer *science*, isn't it? You'll still be a scientist."

It was a stupid joke, and Julia didn't laugh. They walked the last half of the bridge in silence.

They were polite to each other that night in the apartment, saying "Excuse me" and "Thank you" as they scooted around each other in the cramped space made even smaller by the fabrics and other textiles that draped from the walls and coat racks. This was Esther's first apartment. Esther's roommate worked in fashion and had agreed, for fifty bucks, to stay somewhere else that weekend so Julia could have her room. Rooney appeared in Esther's thoughts for the first time in a long time that night, given the superficial parallels between then and now: an apartment, a phantom third person, a summer.

After they watched a movie, Julia announced she was going to bed. In her room, Esther crawled out the window onto the fire escape and lit a cigarette, a habit she'd picked up from Bobby. She had planned on telling Julia about it but now wasn't so sure. Her building was next to a KFC. It was ugly from the front, but the back faced the backs of other buildings, row homes and low rises, separated by patchy, overgrown yards, many of them filled with junk. Everyone on the block seemed to have the same idea about blinds, that they were unnecessary when windows didn't peer onto the street.

So far, without even trying, she'd seen a Saint Bernard poking its snout out from one of those protruding window guards. There were two kids, brothers, Esther assumed, who also had the impulse to spy, their eyes turning into four black holes where they made hand binoculars against the glass. She felt bad for them, that while she could see them they couldn't see her. She made sure of it by turning off all the lights. One time, she saw a woman chopping carrots with small, careful motions and felt moved by the task, the slowness of it and the patience that it required. It was the kind of thing she would have told

Julia before, what she saw and how it made her feel.

The night was dry and still. Ambient sounds of the city drifted to her ears, car alarms and reggaeton cut by an occasional human voice. She took a drag from her cigarette and wondered if those children could see the small ember pulsing, like a message in the dark.

The next day, their last before Julia flew back, they wanted to try a pizza spot that had gotten rave reviews on the Upper West Side. Directions had said it would be right next to the station, but there was no sign for pizza when they got off the train, even after they had circled the block. A group of guys was huddled near the station stairwell, standing in such a way as to appear aware of their collective maleness, posturing rigidly with hunched backs, hands inside pockets, not too close to each other.

"They said we got off a stop early," Esther said to Julia, who'd hung back. "It's just a fifteen-minute walk down Amsterdam. They invited us to get a drink with them just now." Esther rolled her eyes. "Apparently even a look in their direction counts as flirting."

Julia shrugged. "It sounds like they were just trying to be nice."

For some reason, it was this that did Esther in, this generous read on a circumstance involving strangers.

She felt like a child, like she had just been scolded in public. Like a child she lashed out.

"What's wrong?"

Julia said nothing, her eyes darting from side to side.

"Why have you been so depressed on this trip, and why are you acting like we didn't used to shit on guys all the time? What am I missing?"

They stood blinking in each other's faces.

"I'm sorry I've been distant," Julia said at last, looking away. "I know how much this trip means to you, to us, but to be honest, the timing couldn't have been worse. I'm really busy right now trying to change my life. You can understand how stressful that is."

It was such an open and honest response that Esther didn't know what to say. She was about to say never mind and let it go, when Julia cut her off.

"But it's not like you haven't been difficult. You go on about your plans, *your plans*, where your life's headed. Meanwhile it's like you're stuck in college. You talk about those years like they were the best of our lives, when they weren't. At least I hope they aren't. I don't like who I was back then, always looking down on people, and I'm trying to be different now, but you won't let me. Sometimes I think you don't want me to have friends besides you.

"In college, you kept me separate from the other groups you were part of. And I know it's not all your fault. I know I'm to blame for acting like I was above it all, but deep down I wanted to be included. I think you knew that but liked keeping me apart."

Esther hadn't known that Julia wished to be included. She could admit she enjoyed having Julia all to herself, but she'd never thought of it as keeping her apart. They had been apart together.

"After college, you never seemed that interested in my life."

"That's not fair," Esther said. "All those times we fantasized about making our lives here, and now here we are, and you've been nothing but sour."

"How come you never asked about Steven? You were so mean about him when we broke up."

Esther recalled the furniture. "Are you defending the person who broke your heart?"

A taxi groaned, bouncing over the potholed street. It was true she hadn't thought Steven was anything special from what Julia had told her. She had labeled him an Alcoholic but had done the same to her own sweet Bobby, whom she would realize she loved only after he moved on from her. She thought the same of all men. They hadn't known when they started the game that Hemingway himself was an alcoholic. The irony only made the game more poignant, proving not one of them was worthy.

"I haven't said much about John because I know you'll judge him. You'll write him off as simple. Meanwhile your thing, whatever it is, with Bobby—you might think it's fun leading him on, but to me it just sounds childish."

A few people happened to catch Esther's gaze as they walked by. Afterward they walked faster.

"I reached out to Rooney a few weeks ago," said Julia. "I called her, and told her I was sorry for treating her the way we did. She was our friend. She introduced us to each other, and we discarded her. Why? Why did we do that?"

She started to cry, but not like she had on the phone following the breakup with Steven. This was measured, almost mannered, hardly any sound.

"We were nineteen," Esther said quietly. What she really thought was that in order to solidify their friendship, it had been necessary to cut ties that had become secondary.

"What did Rooney say?"

"She's married and lives in Dallas now. She thanked me for the apology and said we should get coffee if I'm ever in town. She invited you as well, but I told her you left Texas."

Julia dabbed below her eyes using her wrists. Esther wanted to scream. She'd been tricked. She was being held accountable to terms she never agreed to, and now, as usual, Julia was getting her way. She was *judging* her. For all her talk of wanting to be different, she was still the same mean girl she always was, only now the rules had changed. She had changed them.

"Have fun with your new best friend I guess," Esther said. "You and Rooney and your attorney husbands can get together in your big houses to talk about the latest drama in the PTA."

Julia scoffed, a flash of her old self. "This is what I mean, see?" she said. "You think that kind of life is beneath you."

She looked up at the sky, and without thinking Esther did the same. The clouds between buildings were faint wisps, as though done in a flick of a painter's brush. She recalled waking up next to Julia on the floor of the apartment they had shared that first summer. Her neck had been stiff for days afterward.

"At some point we have to grow up. You can put it off for as long as you want, but at some point it's going to happen."

"What about New York then?" Esther asked. Later, she would be embarrassed to have been clinging to an idea of a future that Julia had clearly abandoned. "Will you be looking for jobs here when it's time?"

Julia opened her mouth right as a train was pulling into the station. The ground beneath them shook. The pummeling grew gradually louder.

"You're right," Esther said, before she could change her mind. "I was ashamed of you. It's why I never included you with the others."

She was lying. Julia had always been astute, but it turned out she was not ruthless. It was Esther who could follow a judgment to its end. This meant she would be alone again.

"Maybe it's best if we forget we were ever friends."

She didn't wait to see Julia's reaction before looping around and down to catch the subway. At the apartment, she left Julia's things in the hallway on the landing.

The KFC was gone. A café had replaced it. It was a nice day, hot but not as humid as it had been. Families were out. A man sat at a table by himself and ate a sandwich with perfect posture.

The street was quieter. The building's edifice, which she once found old and hideous, looked quaint now beside the café, with its Renaissance Revival flourishes carved out of limestone, contrasting with faded brick.

She remembered the red lit-up awning from when she used to walk under it to get home. At night the light was so bright, teenagers set up a living area underneath, complete with chairs and a complicated sound system.

After leaving Julia's things, she'd climbed out to the fire escape but left every single light in the apartment on, so that Julia would know she was home. Julia would ring the bell, and Esther would open the door. That was how she pictured it. They would both say sorry.

It got later, and darker, until the apartment was like a fishbowl. Anyone on that back-facing block would have had a clear view into her room, which still had that drab flavor of a college dorm. There was a bed, a bulletin board above it, holding pictures of her and Julia and little notes they'd written one another over the years, trimmed in hearts and stars.

She dismantled it methodically, thinking about that woman cutting carrots as she set each item carefully on her desk, catching a thumbtack before it rolled away, stacking photos with other photos, scraps of paper with other scraps of paper—not sure yet what she would do with it all. Those kids with their hand binoculars would get a show tonight, or maybe someone else was in the mood to watch. They might wonder what she was doing, and under their supervision she would feel like she did with Julia, how she'd felt with Bobby in the rare, brief moments when she let herself be loved by him. How she'd felt as a child when her father pushed her on the swing. She laughed louder and more high-pitched when she saw what pleasure it gave him to see her happy. In front of someone else, one comes alive.

Any Good Wife

S he cracked an egg into a bowl deftly using one hand, wearing the blue apron she always wore, which had become part of the image of her in his mind. Her hair was pulled back. Tight black curls exploded out of a scrunchie, haloed in the warm kitchen light. From his desk, which was also the dining table, Ping watched her.

She'd come home last week with a perm and said, "Lao gong, do you like it?" using her fingers to fluff the back.

"Your hair," he'd replied, stunned by its size.

"Like it?" she asked again.

"The style is popular here."

"Exactly," she said, and smiled, specks of red lipstick on her teeth.

The curls gave her an invigorated, healthy look. Only seven months ago, they'd taken a bus from their hometown to Xi'an, and then a train to Beijing, where they boarded their flight to the US. Ailian had, for the entire journey, leaned her head against a window, eyes closed while awake. Her face was a shade of gray. Her hair, straight back then, was clumped into sections by sweat.

"Is your wife okay?" a concerned ah yi had asked on the train.

He'd replied that she was fine, adding quickly that she was

prone to motion sickness.

In the kitchen, Ailian tuned the radio to a rock station. She beat the eggs in tempo with chopsticks.

"How was work today?" she asked.

Ping glanced down at his papers. "Busy," he said. He shuffled his pens around and swiped off his glasses. "Dr. Hunt has me grading undergraduate work."

"Aren't you supposed to be helping him with research?" She set the bowl down and brushed a loose curl from her forehead using the fleshy part of her thumb. "You said his grant went through."

Ailian was attentive. She retained the minutiae from one conversation and applied it in the next, and while Ping knew to be appreciative, at times he wished their lives existed in separate planes, intersecting and overlapping only in practical matters—a car or a house, or children.

"He has his other graduate students helping him for now," he said. "I'll be useful to him once he begins writing."

The oven sounded, a flat, woeful note that startled them both.

There was hardly room for her ankles when she opened the oven. The backs of her legs touched the island. The kitchen was small like the rest of the apartment, the floor plan designed to imitate wealth—each section a distinct territory, separated by elliptical archways—resulting in an uneconomical use of space. She grabbed a mitt and used it to fan the heat. Dinner was a green bean casserole, the third casserole she'd made this week. Dessert, Ping guessed from the egg, would be a cake of some sort.

Her obsession began in July, about a month after they arrived in Tucson. The semester hadn't started, so every morning, when downtown was quiet except for the occasional truck roaring by, they went on a long walk, not sure how else to pass time. The walks were hardly scenic. Advertisements and signs for small businesses were scattered all along East Speedway Boulevard. Blasts of heat dried out their eyes and made their lips crack. They spoke only to say how hot it was or to remark at a billboard: *Saxon's Sandwich Shoppes—OUR FOOD IS RATED G / GREAT.* Summers in Xi'an were just as hot but also humid, a lot of breathing in other people's sweat. He was glad at least to be rid of the wetness.

On one of the return trips, Ailian found an old copy of *Good Housekeeping* lying on the shoulder of the road, faded from baking under the sun. She picked up the magazine carefully, as though she recognized the face on the cover, and held it in front of her at arm's length.

"So lovely," she said, "this woman. What do you think?" She craned her neck around, birdlike.

Behind Ailian, Ping's glasses were sliding down, but he didn't bother adjusting them. He tilted his head back to see. The woman was by all standards attractive, but for all he knew, she could've been the absentminded cashier who rang up their groceries at El Rancho. Big hay-colored hair, wide brown eyes. A nose with an upward tilt at the bottom. Each feature was striking on its own, but together they formed a generic blankness.

"Beautiful," he said.

Ailian turned to the woman again. She flicked a blade of yellow grass from the woman's left ear, then rolled the magazine up and carried it home in her armpit.

He'd expected the pages to be filled with leggy women in bright clothing, ads for beauty products; he hadn't known there would be recipes and tips on how to *Make dinner easy, economical, and edible, too! For the whole family!* Ailian began working in the kitchen with a frenzied willfulness that had been absent when dinners were rice with vegetables and tofu, purchased from the one Chinese grocer in a barrio on the other side of town, or even pork cutlet, which she'd said was a favorite dish of hers and a specialty—the recipe a family heirloom—but which she prepared and ate like it was a chore.

In August, shortly after the start of the fall term, he came home to a dome on the table, the color and translucence of urine. Lettuce and small tomatoes made a wreath around the perimeter. Inside the dome, sliced radishes and shredded cabbage were suspended in space.

"The food is trapped?" he'd asked, wondering if this was a joke or a game. "How do I get to it?"

"You eat the whole thing," Ailian said, looking pleased with herself. "It's lemon-flavored. They call it *Jell-O*."

If he could go back and change one thing, he would have made sure the operation was scheduled earlier. Ailian had tried, but the only appointment available fell three days before their train to Beijing. They had gone into Xi'an proper, where the whole thing was dealt with in an afternoon. The process was swift and impersonal; no one asked to see a marriage license, which Ping had been prepared to show. It was selfish, he knew, this desire to rearrange the past, but he wanted to forget Ailian's wan skin, all the times she'd excused herself for the bathroom on the plane. These images had no place in his present but invaded it nonetheless.

The baby had not been his. That had never been a question. They met only twice before they decided, or rather, their families decided, it was a sensible match. Ping had been admitted to the University of Arizona as a visiting scholar. The government was funding only a handful of students that year, just over three thousand, the newspapers said, and of course he was one of them. First in his class at Qing Hua University. First in his class his entire academic life.

He was aware of the politics, what they would mean to each other until they meant something else over time, if they were lucky something more. Ailian: a way into a conventional life his parents had worried he would never have on account of his shyness and the pockmarks disfiguring his round, dark face. Ping, an opportunity: Ailian's way out of the dogshit place that China had become in the last twenty-some years. That was how his father-in-law described the country when he was drunk, as dogshit or sometimes horseshit. The rumor was that their family had been wealthy before the Communist Party took over, acres upon acres of land in their name. His parents knew this and, despite his reassurances that his stipend was enough to support two comfortably and still have some money to send home, they exploited it for a hefty dowry, to make up for the fact that they were sending their only child away with very little besides a wife. Ping and Ailian had to travel light, so the dowry came mostly in cash. They received none of the usual household amenities: dining sets, towels, satin bedsheets—everything in red for good fortune.

Ping cleared the table and stacked his pens and papers on the counter behind him. Ailian divided the casserole with a spatula. The smell of creamy mushroom, which once disgusted him, now stirred his appetite. He held his plate out to her as she scraped a piece from the side, testing it twice for balance before flipping it down, revealing a brown, crispy bottom.

He had never told Ailian about the adjustment period. Besides Jell-O salad, he'd also suffered vegetable salads, potato salads, tri-color pasta salads.... Everything was smothered in a thick white sauce called mayonnaise. It would be weeks before she discovered the casserole on page 27 of *Good Housekeeping*, a more recent issue: *The quickest way to feed a hungry family! A throw-back to America's golden age!*

Ping had fetched the issue out of the secretary's trash. He was tired of cold leaves for dinner and thought a new magazine might give Ailian some ideas, add a little variety to his diet. He'd left it on the island next to the old, battered one, hoping his gesture would be seen as thoughtful, not critical.

The casserole quickly became her go-to choice for dinner,

prized, he was sure, as *Good Housekeeping* advertised, for its efficiency. Into a glass dish she dumped cans of vegetables and beans, heavy cream, a bag of thawed peas, and on the rare occasion that she used fresh produce, a diced onion went into the mix. She added fruit too sometimes, pineapples or peaches soaked in syrupy water.

His stomach revolted. He hadn't yet learned the term "lactose intolerant," but he figured it must be the dairy, or the preservatives—how long could food really keep in a can? Frozen?

As he sat on the toilet, his thoughts would drift to his mother's hand-cut noodles; cumin and chili lamb stuffed in a pocket of bread, sold in the street alongside whole chickens roasting on a spit. Then a wave of pain would strike his abdomen, and he couldn't think about food anymore.

By October, Ailian had gained confidence in the kitchen. She began preparing more meat. Pork chops, lamb chops, chicken legs, wings—they all tasted basically the same, seasoned with salt and pepper. The first time Ping cut into a steak, he let out a whimper. He wasn't expecting the blood.

"They call it *medium rare*," said Ailian. "It's safe to eat, don't worry."

Ping resumed cutting until he saw red in the center.

"It's safe," she assured him again.

He found out about the pregnancy in the courtyard connecting their villages, only hours after he'd arrived home from campus, having completed his final Beijing semester.

Ailian's voice was stern and matter-of-fact.

"I'm pregnant," she said.

He felt tired and remembered that he did not sleep well on the train. He'd dreamed of his flight to San Francisco, boarded completely by passengers who were people from his hometown. Behind Ailian, dusk was settling in, the remnants of light casting a persimmon glow over the mountains. He'd thought she was going to call off the marriage and had prepared himself accordingly. He wouldn't beg or plead with her, he'd decided, walking here. He would honor her wishes, save what little dignity he had left, and travel to the States alone.

He took his glasses off and cleaned them using his breath and shirt sleeve.

"I'm pregnant, Ping," she said again, this time with less resolve. It almost sounded like a question.

He put his glasses on and replayed the day's events. That morning, before he even set his bags down, his mother looked up from her cutting board and said to him, "You're back. I have something for you." She set her cleaver aside and pranced like a deer into the bedroom, wiping her hands on her pants as she went. She came back with a small basket of lychee.

"From your fiancée," she said. "She told me she knows they're your favorite."

The cheeriness in his mother's voice, laced with something coy and teasing, embarrassed him.

"She is already making efforts to please you. She already thinks the way any good wife does."

The way his mother was holding the basket—to her side with one hand grasping the handle, the other supporting the bottom, like the contents inside were heavy and precious—she may as well have been presenting him with gold.

He waited the rest of the morning for his mother to retreat for her afternoon nap. In the kitchen, he turned the basket over and watched as the fruit scattered, careening around the countertop, the sound some of them made as they hit the floor no louder than that of a fat raindrop. His mother stirred in the bedroom and fell back asleep.

There was a note at the bottom of the basket, just as he'd dreaded. It had been folded four times and felt like a pebble in his hand, compact and light. The instructions in it said: *Meet me at five at the west entrance by the lions. I have something important to tell you.*

So far, everything was going according to her plan. Ping still couldn't find any words. He pictured her writing the note at night, after her parents and siblings had gone to sleep, folding the note into a tiny square and placing it into a basket that she then filled to the brim with lychee. That morning, she must have ridden her bike three miles up two steep hills to drop the basket off with her soon-to-be mother-in-law, telling her it was a gift for him.

He understood it was the only way to ensure the secrecy of their meeting, but he considered now whether she knew he would instantly recognize the gift as subterfuge. If that was true, then it was sad; it meant they both knew such romance was beyond them. Or had she thought he would embrace the gesture as it appeared? Did she think he would enjoy the lychee and her flirtation, only to realize at the end that he was a fool?

Which version of her was worse? Which version of him?

He'd savored the fruit anyway, sucking on the white flesh until there was not one left.

"I'm getting an abortion," she said. "You don't have to come with me."

The sky was fading to indigo. A loose braid hugged the curve of Ailian's neck. Her lips and cheeks were rouged, not totally natural, though the shades of pink mixed for a convincing imitation of a face in full flush. She smelled like chrysanthemum. He had to wonder if she did it on purpose, made herself beautiful to soften the impact, but he didn't feel pain or even jealousy, just a hollowness inside. That was how he knew, if there had been any doubt before, that he didn't love her.

"If you're going to get an abortion anyway, why bother telling me?" he said.

"It's the right thing to do," she replied.

"Where was this morality when you were with another man?"

A meanness grew inside of him, pulling him into a feeling of ownership. His heart beat fast in the back of his throat.

"I was caught in a different morality then," she said. "I loved him."

"And now?"

She held his stare. Everything was still except for her bangs twitching in the breeze. He looked away. He felt himself coming down, losing control as quickly as he'd gained it.

"What about him?" she said. "I'm marrying you. I'm leaving this place."

A child rang the bell on his bicycle, shouting after his brother—"Ge! Wait up!"—and Ping found his familiar surroundings suddenly strange, like he was seeing it all for the first time. Every detail was extraordinary in its dullness. The ground of the courtyard was covered as it always was in a tan powdery dirt. Men smoked cigarettes, their pant legs rolled up to their knees, exposing glistening shins, sweaty from a long day of readying sorghum for harvest. Women walked in slow side-to-side rocks. Baskets of peaches and dried dates hung from their wrists. The commonness added insult, ill-suited as it was for this half-tragedy.

It was mid-January now, and he and Ailian had fallen into a steady routine centered around mealtimes. In the morning, he would leave his wife in the kitchen, scrubbing at the bottom of a pan.

"I'm leaving," he would say.

She would pause and consider him, as though she'd forgotten who he was, as though it were possible to look away, and look back, and find oneself in a completely different life.

"Goodbye, lao gong!" she would say hurriedly.

She smiled when she reminded him to walk slowly.

He attended classes and seminars and didn't think about his wife again until noon. His lunches had become standardized. Every day she packed him either a sandwich or a wrap sealed in thin plastic, which he liked for their utilitarian quality, how the ingredients stacked neatly on top of one another. He developed a habit of peeking inside before taking the first bite, wondering how she decided today whether it was going to be turkey or ham, lettuce or spinach, white or orange cheese. He ate in the common area outside the math and sciences building, on one of the worn couches. Whenever someone he knew walked by, he pretended to be too busy eating to notice.

He came home in the evenings around five or six to her mixing something or draining a can, wearing that same blue apron. She would say, "Dinner's almost ready," to which he wouldn't reply, choosing instead to loosen the collar on his shirt, drape his tie over a chair.

The first time they slept together, on their wedding night, the growth in Ailian's body not yet removed, he got hard by imagining himself as the other man. This allowed him to desire her. He hadn't formalized it before, the tickling irony. It was love that had nearly ruined their future, and the lack of love that made it work in the end, permitting them to move forward. Ailian was at the island now, on her toes, piping icing. They were having cake for dessert, like he'd guessed.

He was on his third serving of casserole and taking his time, making careful, even demarcations with his fork. Ailian had chosen a small corner piece and had finished it in under a minute. She ate fast and little these days, eager to be away from him and back in the kitchen, it seemed, though he couldn't complain. It was better than when they would sit at the table for what felt like hours, shoveling rice into their mouths with their bowls up to their faces, tearing at the pork cutlet in an effort to fill the quiet. Now the food was worse, but the atmosphere was better. They still ate in silence, but soon Ailian would become chatty again, now that she was back in the kitchen.

Spreading the icing with a butter knife, she asked Ping the

same question she asked every night, the same question she'd had about her hair.

"Do you like it, lao gong?"

He nodded and said dinner was delicious.

"Good," she replied.

Her efforts always amounted to this exchange of niceties.

At the table, she pushed his used plate aside.

"Devil's cake," she said, as she slid the whole thing in front of him. "With fudge icing."

Tiny air bubbles were lodged into the cake's surface, this *icing* Americans liked to put on every dessert. The sugar would no doubt give him a headache. Mooncakes and red bean buns had hinted at sweetness. Here, the flavor reached its full potential.

She leaned over him and began cutting a single slice. He felt like a child sitting there, waiting for her. When she stood up, her breast grazed the side of his head.

"You need silverware," she said. "Wait."

There was a hop in her step; she was almost skipping into the kitchen. Her curls bounced as her slippers slapped the tile. After some rummaging, she came back with a clean fork. The piece of cake nearly fell over when she plated it. She used her index finger to stabilize.

"Go on, take a bite," she said, sucking the icing off her finger.

"You don't want any?"

"I'll have some later. I want to know what you think first." She pulled a chair up close to his. "It's a cake from Betty Crocker."

"Who?"

She waved the question away. "A woman who knows all the secrets about cooking and baking." She crossed her legs energetically. "She makes being in the kitchen easier for women like me."

Picking up the fork, Ping wondered exactly what type of woman Ailian was. She had been with another man during their engagement, but if he hadn't loved her, hadn't even known her then, how bad was the transgression, really? He often critiqued himself within these same parameters, asking if he was, if not necessarily the right man, then at least a good man for his wife.

He was starting to believe it was all a matter of playing pretend, and that a person's commitment to pretending was all that was needed to make any relationship last. Apart from his wife, he put this into practice. He attempted solidarity with his professors and peers—*How's it going?* a simple line he always made a mess of, saying *How it's going?* instead—but he could sense their discomfort at his wish to be included, their tight lips and wandering eyes, their bodies that angled away. He had filled almost an entire notebook up with American colloquialisms but so far hadn't used one.

She nudged his plate.

"What are you waiting for?"

If there was a way to quantify the qualities between them, he knew the result would come out positive on her side, proving that she was a better person. She pretended to love him, and this was a show of kindness because it was sincere. She was steadfast in their new life. She never seemed sorry over what had happened, neither the problem nor its resolution. Instead she'd found a way to make herself useful.

Sometimes over dinner, when Ailian's wifeliness became almost unbearable, he contemplated whether it was cruel that he hadn't urged her to keep the child, offering to raise it as his own. What would they be like with something like that between them? He would feel ashamed almost immediately for indulging in this impossible fantasy, and beyond that, for allowing his imagination to grant him a feeling of goodness that he knew he had not earned.

Each time, he concluded he was making things unnecessarily complicated. All they could do now was play their parts, achieve a likeness to love, and hope it would be enough. Ping sunk his fork into the spongy loaf. Not hungry, he ate.

Sister Machinery

There were three of us before there were two, before our sister got hit by a car when I was twelve and Pearl had just turned sixteen. Em was fourteen when she died. Our ages are prominent because a few months later, Pearl got her driver's license and we—Pearl, me, Ma, Ba—went to the Olive Garden to celebrate. Pearl drove. At the restaurant, Ba lied and told the waiter it was Pearl's birthday, and the staff brought out a little lava cake with a single fat candle. "Make a wish!" Ba said. Ma looked up from the table stiffly, her face like one of those dolls you tilt back and forth to make the eyes open and close. Like those dolls, it didn't seem like she was seeing anything. From that day on, Pearl was hardly ever home. She drove a used silver Toyota, and one could say this was all very macabre given our circumstance, and given that sixteen-year-olds have higher crash rates than drivers of any other age. But our parents had forced us to read *Girls and Women Who Lead and Succeed*. We'd discussed the book for weeks over dinner. Fear, Ba believed and Ma understood, was no paradigm for success.

Em was the middle sister, which meant once upon a time Ma was pregnant for forever. Ma talked about those years like she loved us most when we were in her womb, flesh of her flesh. "It balanced me," she would say. "I became a more balanced person. I ate a banana in the morning and an apple in the afternoon." This was Ma: prone to repetition and self-lacerating for not eating enough fruit. "And you guys loved vinegar," she would add, her gaze bouncing off of us in a triangle, in the order in which we were born. "Not the clear stuff, the Chinese stuff. I took it straight from the bottle."

We felt a little jealous of our fetal selves, I guess, so one overcast Sunday morning, when our parents were still asleep and church programming was the only thing on TV, we poured the brown liquid into a bowl and sat huddled on the kitchen floor, between the stove and the sink. We were six-eight-ten. The warm linoleum stuck to our legs. We passed the bowl around, one slurping mouthful after another, until Ba walked in and said, "What are you three up to?"

Here was the situation: Pearl belonged to Ba, Em belonged to Ma, and I belonged to my sisters. Our family photos are proof of this. The earliest one was taken at a portrait studio in Walmart, us three looking like playground chalk in our white pantyhose and doily pastel rompers, cut and sewn from the same fabric by our laolao who lived in California. I'm a baby, front and center; Em and Pearl are behind me, leaning in so that their shoulders touch; Ma is staggered behind Em, and Ba is on the other side behind Pearl. Apparently the photographer did thirty-six takes before he got one of me smiling. "It was flapping his arms and jumping that did it," Pearl told me and Em. "That's how he got the shot." She imitated him on the platform of the stairs in our house, above which the photo was hung, and Em and I had yelled "Caw! Caw!" from the bottom, in what we imagined to be the sound of a frantic chicken. Pearl was five in the photo, the only one of us old enough to retain the memory. It was tickling for me to know that as a baby, I'd had the power to inflict ridiculousness on a grown man.

My parents don't remember me being difficult at all; in fact, when I used to ask them about us, they seemed not to recall anything in detail. "You guys were the sweetest," Ba would say, about the Walmart Incident and everything else. *Selective amnesia* Pearl had called it, after she became a teenager and found our parents unbearably treacle. It's something I've been thinking about, wondering whether happiness really does dull specificity.

So from left to right, it went: Ma, Em, me, Pearl, Ba. Like a pack of migrating geese. It was as though the Walmart photographer had somehow imprinted this arrangement on us, casting us in our relationships. Ba ran errands with Pearl, and since he was always running errands, they were always together. He bought her slushies that turned her lips blue and told her she would be the first ever Chinese American president, and that was what Pearl put in the Hopes and Dreams section of her fifth-grade yearbook. He told Em she could be the second and me that I could be third, but the same ambition on us felt like a consolation—so Em put "Olympian" in her fifth-grade yearbook, and I put the generic "world peace" in mine.

Ma, on the other hand, yearned for touch, which she didn't get often from Ba because he was constantly on the move. This was Ba: going going going, ever striving toward some small greatness— a new appliance or tool, his succulents, a class on motivational speaking. Perhaps her longing had to do with that sense of oneness she'd felt with us during her pregnancies. It was Em who gave her the most, every evening laying her head in Ma's lap, the white glow from the television pulsing on their foreheads. Ma would brush Em's hair with one hand and reach the other into a bowl of strawberries, occasionally dipping one into Em's mouth.

And this was me: less distinct at twelve than Pearl and Emily had been at that age because my parents' expectations came to me diluted through my siblings. I learned everything a little late, Em and Pearl realizing suddenly each time that I still couldn't tie my shoes or swim or fold shirts, and then working together to teach me. By the time we were four-six-eight, Ma and Ba had stable, well-paying jobs at Dell and IBM. They'd moved into a larger house in a newer part of Plano, a community with two swimming pools, trails, roundabouts, trees that flowered in the spring. They loved me easily, without the clinginess brought about by worry, which they'd each exhausted on one child already. I would have clothes, food, extracurricular activities, they were sure. They didn't even have to worry about friends because I had sisters.

Whenever it came time to take a picture, no matter the occasion or where we were next to each other, we would scramble to make our V. Graduations, recitals, ski trips; when Pearl placed second at the middle school science fair; Christmases, Chinese New Years, Enchanted Rock; in the hospital after Em broke her arm doing a kickflip and got a hot-green cast we all signed; Disney World, Disneyland; when I lost my last baby tooth, which Ma thought was a big deal for everyone. "Our baby is no longer a baby," she kept saying, and repeated, "Our baby is growing up." In that photo we're seven-nine-eleven, and I'm stretching my palm to the camera. The photo came out saturated, though, so you can't really see the small groovy molar, only some bits of red where there was blood. In our home, the tripod sat permanently by the fireplace. Out in the world, we were that family that was always saying, "Excuse me, would you mind?"

Except for at Olive Garden, when Pearl didn't want to.

"Why not?" Ba said in the booth. The metallic-pink camera hung from his wrist. "You can drive now. That's something to celebrate."

"I just don't want to, okay?"

"She doesn't want to, Eric," said Ma, still with that wooden gaze.

"Jessica, what about you?"

"Ba, why are you asking Jessie?"

I said I didn't want to, to align myself with Pearl, knowing that Em was normally her accomplice. In the past, no one would have asked for my opinion.

"See? There. End of story. Let's go home."

With that, Pearl slid out of her seat. She left me with them and walked out of the restaurant, her long straight hair trembling as she clopped through the parking lot in black boots, a gift from Ma on Pearl's actual sixteenth birthday months ago. Olive Garden must have been when it started: we had gone from three to one and one, and that somehow wasn't the same as two.

I said I needed to pee and shuffled out of the booth, feeling Pearl's warmth as I passed where she'd been sitting. When I got back, Ma and Ba were hissing, speaking loud and soft at the same time. I listened with my back against the corner.

"You were wrong for pushing the photo," said Ma.

"I don't think so."

"Why are you acting like what happened didn't happen?"

"What happened happened, but we have to help them move on."

"We have to let them feel."

"It's important to maintain structure."

"It's her first milestone without her sister."

"There will be many more. Will she acknowledge none of them?"

"You're impatient. You always have been. You were when I met you, and you still are."

"Can we not discuss what we were like when we met right now, please?"

A waiter walked past me with breadsticks and I thought, for the first time, of when my parents weren't Ma and Ba but Clarissa and Eric, two people who were once strangers. It didn't seem possible. Their silence was cut by tinny percussion, Ma scraping leftovers into to-go containers, exaggerating her movements because she was upset. Plastic grunted, lids being shut, followed by silence again before Ba's glasses clattered onto the table.

———————

They say it's common when a person gets hit by a car for their shoes to stay exactly where they were on the ground just before the moment of impact. Emily's skateboard was intact, not a single scratch on the deck. She skated mongo, meaning she pushed with her front foot instead of her back, which meant that her board was always a little ahead of her.

I picture it when I can't sleep. Rolling on by itself, jittery without the extra weight.

None of us was there when it happened, but Ma and Ba brought the board home along with Em's right shoe, while the left, they said, was nowhere to be found. We pass the intersection on our way to Home Depot—me and Ba now, instead of Ba and Pearl—and every time I can't help but look. I know Ba is looking too. I'm afraid of seeing it, the checkered black-and-purple Vans, seeing it and knowing that all the parts of her are accounted for, which would make her truly gone, while right now, a piece of her is still out there.

I was getting a glass of water when I heard "Shit!" and "Shitshitshit!" coming from outside. After the Olive Garden, Pearl went to a friend's house. To study for a test, she'd told us, though it was well past midnight now, and Ma and Ba were asleep. It was the first time I ever heard her cuss.

When she saw me, she muttered, "Oh hey," and closed the front door walking backward, staring at the ground. She raised her keys to hang them on the wall before snatching them back and plunging them into her jacket pocket.

I asked her what was wrong.

"What?"

"You're acting weird."

"I'm not."

"Okay."

"Fine, I scratched the car a little bit, okay? Don't tell."

"What happened?"

"Nothing. I was taking Bullock Hollow a little fast, and you know how winding it is, how it's narrow and two ways."

I knew Bullock Hollow was a shortcut to the high school on days when the traffic was bad. I also knew it conveniently avoided the intersection.

"A car came out of nowhere, headlights turning everything white, and I got scared for a second. I was going downhill and didn't think I could make the turn, so I hit the brakes and veered into the railing. The right side got dragged a little, that's all. No big deal. I usually park on the other side of the street anyway, so Ma and Ba won't see the damage unless they walk around."

"I won't say anything," I said, hurt that she was trying to convince me.

"Cool. I know I've been busy. I miss you."

"Miss you too."

"I'm hungry."

"Me too," I said, even though I wasn't. "I can make us something."

Pearl frowned. She walked past me into the living room, her voice trailing behind her. "When did you learn how to cook?"

Before Em was sent flying by a car going sixty, she used to come home from school, let her backpack fall off wherever, and stick her head deep into the fridge, as though being sucked in by the light. Pearl liked food just fine but was generally not driven by appetite. I was somewhere in the middle, which meant that when I got hungry I was only proactive enough to go looking for Ma or Em. Em had shown me her basics. Guacamole. Roasted carrots with cinnamon. "So you don't starve," she'd said. "You need to know how to make your own snacks."

Ma liked to follow recipes. She would buy ingredients in precisely the stated proportions, but then when it came time to prep she would look up from a produce bag and yell something like, "TOMATOES?" and Em would yell back, from wherever she was in the house, "GONE-I-YATE-THEM!"

Our meals were often a surprise. Apple pie that turned out to be half apple, half Korean pear. A salad that was hardly more than oily lettuce. When we were nine-eleven-thirteen, we ate hummus on spoons like yogurt because Em had finished all the bread, and that same morning we took our smoothies at room temperature because when Ma had looked, there were no bananas in the freezer.

Em's Munchies Incidents, we called these. Our Ma would learn to compensate by buying extra, you would think, but she didn't. She accepted the absent ingredients as a creative exercise, or maybe practice in case of an emergency. If something crucial had gone missing, what could you use as a substitute? What could you do without?

I carried our grilled cheeses to the table, and Pearl brought out a desk lamp from her room. "Mood lighting," she said, and angled the circular head to the ceiling, which I never would've thought to do because I wasn't Pearl: attentive to detail and capable of wonder. The light fell over us like a fine net, touching us softly while we ate.

"I'll show you a trick," I said. It was Em's trick. When I came back from the kitchen with Ma's chili oil, there was only a wedge of Pearl's sandwich left. I wafted the clear dispenser under her nose, smelling the star anise.

Pearl pulled her face into her neck and said, "No."

"It's good, I promise."

"Dairy plus Asian-spicy equals diarrhea."

"What's that thing Ba used to say? Unless you'll die, it's worth a try?"

"Horrible advice. There are way worse things than death."

We got quiet. Pearl's features—her quaint knoll of a nose, her apple-shaped lips; Pearl was beautiful—turned dark all of a sudden. I noticed after a while that I was holding my breath, and that the chili oil was still in Pearl's face.

"Remember that time," I said, gripping our moment of togetherness. "We were little, and we drank all that vinegar. Whose idea was that?"

Pearl took a sharp breath and stood up. She became all bright again. "I'm pooped. Ha. I'm going to bed. If you want indigestion, you're on your own. Love you," she said, and kissed my cheek. "Let's talk tomorrow."

But we didn't talk tomorrow, or the next day, or the day after. Through my window, I watched every night as Pearl's car turned in, slowed down. The double flash of the headlights, the doors locking, silhouetting her as she pranced across the yard to the front steps. Weeks went by. No one found out about the car. Ba got a promotion at work. He was always in and out of doors; meanwhile, Ma stayed still. She rinsed grapes at the sink for minutes and was always touching my face, my arms, saying things like, "You know you can talk to me, right?" and then again: "I'm here if you need me."

At night, I wait for Pearl to come to me. Em's skateboard draws circles inside my head. After a while, I peek into her room and find her passed out on her stomach in a wide X, her jacket collar riding up, obscuring half her face. I peel off her socks. I switch off her light.

The Saturday after Pearl's real sixteenth birthday, just ten days before the *Incident* Incident, my sisters tried teaching me how to ride a bike. It was only May, but all of Texas was swept in a record-breaking heat. It had become unseemly, they said, that at twelve I hadn't learned this basic skill. That was the word they'd used, *unseemly*, because every few months we found a new word and would use it mercilessly until we'd rubbed it down so that it lost its luster. Others throughout the years included *preposterous, coy, gruesome, superb.*

They had decided to run alongside me, but the question now was how. We'd been outside for minutes and already our temples were glistening, the space above our lips dotted with sweat. I was between my sisters on the bike, trying to find a good position on the seat. I hobbled on my one foot touching the ground.

"Ma held my handlebars," said Em. "Otherwise you'll go all over the place when you're nervous."

"Ba pushed me from behind. That way the pedals move"— Pearl rolled her index fingers, so fast that they blurred—"and you have enough momentum to steer on your own."

"Let's try both," I said.

Pearl and Em responded together, "At the same time?"

Even though I'd meant one and then the other, I shrugged and said, "Yeah."

We found a long flat stretch of sidewalk two blocks from our house. Pearl was behind me, touching the bike seat and my shoulder. Em was next to me on the other side, one hand on the handlebars, the other on my lower back where I could feel sweat beginning to pool. I shook my helmet head. The straps tickled my chin.

"Ready, Jessie?" said Em.

"No."

"Too bad," said Pearl. "You're old. It's unseemly."

"You're unseemly," I said. "And old."

"Good one," said Pearl.

"On the count of three," said Em. "One, two, THREE."

They pushed. A slow jog at first and then faster. We were running, all legs and wheels, tangled arms, protruding elbows, a single moving entity. How did we look? I wonder. On nights when I'm up waiting for Pearl, I try to picture us. A three-headed creature. A machine.

"You have to pedal!" Em shouted. "Are you pedaling?"

I wasn't. I was laughing. I was hardly even holding onto the bike. Eventually, we came to a crosswalk and stopped. "Let's go back," I said. "We can do this another time." Through harrowed breaths they agreed it was too hot, and together the three of us ran, with me on the bike, all the way back home.

Knowing

We were not connected by blood. He was my mother's best friend's father, and though I never readily recall this detail, his wife had just died, prompting him to leave China and move in with his daughter in America. I was told to call him Yeye. *Grandfather*.

Downpours throughout Texas that summer beat a century-old record and ended the drought that had lasted nearly a decade. The rain came in its variations every week. Abiding drizzles, slanted thunderstorms, fat drops that hit the ground a few at a time, then all at once. It kept me away from my friends and stuck inside, with no one to play with except my little brother. The lake had risen six inches so far and would rise eight more before the summer was over. Until the rain stopped in August, temperatures never reached above 82. Hot, but nothing compared to what we were used to, a heat so oppressive that radios would overheat and shut off, the view in the distance breaking and bending, as though the whole world had gone up in flames.

"What about *sir* or *mister*?" I asked my mother, scratching a fresh mosquito bite on my leg. I had met my grandparents on my father's side only once, in China, and was too young to remember it. The other side, I'd been told, had been dead since before I was born. This person was a stranger to me.

The afternoon was just dipping into evening. We were hanging our clothes to dry in the backyard, glad that the heat wasn't intolerable. Gusts of moist air cooled our sweat and gave the clothes we'd hung a dreadful liveliness, pants and shirts swaying like dismembered body parts.

In front of the clothesline, my mother squinted at me. Tiny goldfish appeared under her eyes, their tails fanning out from the corners to reinforce the symmetry that made her face beautiful and terrifying. I handed her a damp T-shirt from the basket, one of Benny's. Looking away from me, my mother shook it out just once, with such force that the crack—a clean and empty sound—made me jump.

"You will call him Yeye," she said, and clipped the shirt onto the line. Still squinting, she stepped back and examined her work. "That is the Chinese way."

She turned to me, using her hand as a visor. The shadow divided her face diagonally; one half light, one half dark.

I was going into the fifth grade. The district rule was that from fifth grade on, math levels were set. If I didn't test into a higher placement now, there would be no more chances. I would be stuck in regular math until I graduated high school.

"You should be excited," my father said to me the night before my first lesson. He was leaning on the kitchen island, shuffling almonds like dice around in his hand. "This Yeye was a professor at Bei Da before the revolution. Do you know what Bei Da is?" He caught an almond in his mouth and chewed.

I was sitting at the dining table, my right knee up, my left arm hanging over the back of the chair. I shook my head, slowly, to show I was serious. Across from me, Benny was finishing a bowl of ice cream. He scraped at the sides, collecting the melted dregs.

"It's the Harvard of China. Do you know what Harvard is?"

"Yes," I said.

"Me too!" said Benny. He raised his spoon into the air and licked the circumference of his mouth, his tongue, for that moment, its own creature.

Yeye was tall and long-limbed. Tawny skin. Tufts of white hair. His breath smelled of cigarettes and bread gone sour in the mouth. We spoke in Chinese because my Chinese was better than his English.

"Multiplying and dividing fractions is easy," he said. "It's the adding and subtracting that's tricky."

I nodded. He cleared his throat.

"Do you know how to multiply fractions?"

"Bu zhi dao," I said quietly, aware of my accent.

"Okay," he said in English. And then in Chinese, "Let's begin there."

My parents drove me to Yeye's house every morning. He and Ahyi lived across town, in a neighborhood where the houses were short and bright, a menagerie of yellows, pinks, and baby blues. I would eat my breakfast in the car, a piece of toast with peanut butter or a pork baozi, and stare out at the lake as we went over the bridge, imagining that I could see the latest rise in water level with my bare eyes. My lessons were four times a week, Monday through Thursday, 8:30 to noon. When the lesson was over, my mother or father, alternating days, picked me back up during their lunch break and drove me home, where I was expected to complete the homework Yeye had assigned and look after Benny, who was already in accelerated math and got to spend mornings at the Y. He complained about being at the library more than at the pool, which kept being closed that summer.

I would see Yeye as soon as we turned onto the cul-de-sac, sitting with perfect posture on a resin bench on the front porch, thinking contentedly, it seemed, about something far away. Most days, he didn't notice us until I'd already climbed out of the car and shut the door. Only then would he inhale and stand as though pulled up by his breath, smile and wave at me in a way that made me wonder if he'd forgotten about our lesson entirely. Together, Yeye and I would watch the black car round the curve before driving off. I took my time walking up the driveway to meet him.

We didn't use workbooks. Yeye handwrote every equation so that no two were ever the same. He was right: multiplying and dividing fractions was easy. It was the simplification that messed me up. I ended up with large numbers on the top and bottom, earning only half the points.

Yeye slid my worksheet across the table, a 50 circled at the top in faint pencil.

My cheeks prickled. "But my answers aren't really wrong, are they?" When he didn't answer, I met his eyes. "The fractions are the same."

Yeye scooted his chair forward and placed his elbows on the table. He wove his long fingers together, making a hammock for his chin. "The same, yes," he said, "but uglier."

I put my pencil down.

"Think of it this way. Someone is telling you a story, maybe it's something important. They talk and talk, and while you eventually understand what they're getting at, you wish they'd said it in fewer words. You wish they would have stated only exactly what they meant. Math is sort of like that. Numbers, remember, have no end." He paused here to pantomime an explosion. His eyes darted from side to side, as though seeing sparks. "There is always some bigger one. The challenge and beauty of math is in finding the smallest numbers to convey value. The fewest words to convey meaning. Ming bai le ma?"

I thought about saying something smart, like that I wouldn't really mind it if someone told me a story that went on and on. Picking up my pencil, I said, "Ming bai le."

"Tsan le! Shit!" My mother opened the back door and ran outside, her hand-visor up against the rain. "Eileen!" she shouted. "Lao Wang! Benny!" Benny was playing a computer game with headphones on. My father was banging around in the garage. I was in the living room, reading on the sofa. I couldn't even pretend I didn't hear her.

Outside, my mother unclipped the clothes as fast as she could and threw them at me. The rain picked up suddenly, with a loud hiss, and my mother said "shit" some more. Halfway to the end, she began ripping everything down. The line bounced like it was laughing at us.

"It's getting heavy," I said.

"What?" my mother yelled over the rain.

"My arms hurt," I said, louder. "It's getting heavy."

"Take those clothes inside and hang them up."

She draped a pair of my father's corduroys over her forearm.

In the utility room, above the dryer we rarely used, I began hanging the clothes on the rail my father had mounted for this very purpose. I'd been to enough friends' houses by then to know that most families used their dryer, that it was not a frivolous appliance, as I had been led by my mother to believe. I took my time so I wouldn't have to go back outside. The smell of rain soon filled the room, a mineral scent that I knew would linger long after the clothes had dried and turned stiff.

Occasionally, I would catch Ahyi on her way out as I was coming in. I'd known my mother's friend all my life. She was always in a rush, headed somewhere else. Her heels knocked against the peach tile, a beat that slowed when she saw me at the door. She would comb my hair back with three fingers.

"So pretty and well-behaved," she said before grabbing her keys off the wall. "Study hard, okay?"

She winked before putting sunglasses on, her smile the last thing I saw in the door before it was pulled shut.

Only once did the two of them come over.

Inside, Yeye appraised our home, nodding with his hands behind his back.

"Lovely," he said, as his eyes continued to roam.

"Jiang found it for us," said my mother.

She gestured with her head at Ahyi, who was retrieving a tray of takeout from the back seat of her car.

Ahyi didn't cook, and neither did my mother. My father enjoyed preparing food and was good at it, but that was not something Benny or I could appreciate as kids. We looked forward to the restaurant fried rice that Ahyi came with every week. It felt like a treat to eat food from outside, and the rice—high in sodium and harder than how our father made it at home—paired nicely with the soda we were allowed to drink only when Ahyi came over.

My father set his final dish onto the table. Benny was rocking from side to side in his chair. He had trouble staying still when he was hungry. I told him to stop and looked to my mother to affirm me affirming what she would have told Benny herself, were she not distracted by a joke that Ahyi was telling.

"So, the guy goes up to the counter, ready to ask *How much?*, which he'd memorized in Chinese as *hao ma-chi*."

A smile crept onto my mother's face. I was struck by how willing she was to be humored.

"But he panics, and what comes out instead is *Hao chi ma?*"

The adults laughed, with modest raucousness, and turned their attention to the food. I laughed too, not because I found the joke funny but because the Chinese it relied on for the punchline was basic enough that I had understood the joke, and I wanted that to be known.

My mother passed Ahyi my father's signature dish, steamed eggplant topped with raw chilis.

"That's enough," Yeye said to Ahyi. "Save some for other people."

"Eileen?" my father said to me, once he'd finished plating rice for Benny.

My little brother's chin was already shining. His feet kicked involuntarily, the backs of his ankles knocking against the chair's wooden spindle. I told my father I didn't want any.

Ahyi gasped dramatically. "No fried rice for Eileen? Why not?"

I shrugged. I hated that she was calling me out.

"I'm going to have more if you're not having any."

She winked. I said okay.

"What about a soda?" said my mother. She reached to the center of the table and jiggled a can of generic-brand orange Fanta.

I said no thanks and was glad this time when no fuss was made about it.

During dinner, Ahyi brought up the personal lives of Beijing film directors and actresses, whose names I could never remember. My father stayed busy refilling everybody's plates. Benny kept trying to engage me in little games. I kept telling him to go away until he eventually left the table to go play by himself. I watched Yeye eat with extraordinary intention. He chewed loudly and unselfconsciously, with his mouth open. His jaw was like a machine, the intricate workings of which were visible through his skin. Half an hour passed. He ate in one continuous motion.

"Thank you, Wuzi," he said to my father, followed by a hiccup and a soft burp. "That was delicious."

My father gathered everybody's plates and announced that there was work he needed to finish. Around this time, whenever

Ahyi was here, he found some reason to excuse himself, leaving the women alone. It was one of the ritual aspects of the evening that I understood intuitively and had therefore never questioned. Benny invited me again to a game of Legos, and again I rejected him, but this time my mother intervened, standing over me with her head directly blocking the overhead light, encasing her in shadow.

"Why don't you go play with Benny?"

It wasn't a question, but I told her I didn't feel like it.

"Yeye and Ahyi and I have to talk," she said.

"About what?"

"Just old friends catching up."

"I'll be quiet," I offered, thinking she would be impressed by my desire to be in the presence of adults, something I'd never expressed.

"Some other time," my mother said. "Go, be with your brother."

Her tone was firm but not ungentle. I had never asserted myself during these dinners before, and I never would again. But that evening, my suspicion toward my mother had reached a new level, and it seemed unacceptable to me that my father and brother were absent from the table and that I was being asked to leave.

"Why do I have to go? Why do they get to stay?" Yeye, who was seated across from me, appeared as he did on the mornings when I arrived for my lessons: removed. It allowed me to say what I said next, that he did not seem really there.

"He's not my real grandfather."

"Say that again and you are not my daughter."

She spoke with incredible nonchalance, like making a comment about the weather. This chilled me at the same time that it brought heat up to my face. I knew I'd all but undone my earlier attempts to appear grown-up, to prove to her that unlike Benny I wasn't a child anymore, that I, too, could humor her and be taken into her confidence.

"Don't cry, Eileen!" Ahyi said, rounding the table. "Don't cry! It's okay! It's okay!"

They were comforting words, roughened by her delivery.

The two of them exchanged a look. This upset me more because it confirmed that there were things only they shared, that they were keeping from me.

"Come, Eileen." Ahyi grabbed my wrist.

"No!" I shouted.

"Let's go for a walk outside."

"I don't want to go anywhere with you!"

"She's too old to be acting like this," said my mother.

Ahyi was standing between us, facing me. Her back was to my mother.

"Like you were never a kid before," she said, her eyes fixed.

It didn't seem like she was seeing me at all. Her gaze reached all the way through me, and frightened me. She looked so much like Yeye.

She let me go. My skin flashed yellow where her fingers had been. I ran to my room and stayed there until the morning.

My father came to me that night after our guests had left. My mother must have told him what happened. A week later, Ahyi came to dinner without Yeye, with her usual tray of rice, which I ate, and the week after that was the same. "Where's Yeye?" I asked her. She said her father didn't like riding in cars; they made him nauseous. Perhaps that was true. My mother started going over there once a week for dinner, without the rest of us, and I accepted this as punishment for what I had done.

"Your mother, like anyone, is who she has become," my father said, shifting closer to me on my bed. Both of us stared at our feet. "You'll understand one day. Part of loving someone is accepting what you don't know, and what you do know. That is what makes a family."

It's possible he was saying this for himself as much as he was saying it for me. To this day, I have no idea how much he knew, how much my mother told him. Out of respect for them both, I do not ask.

In a month, I was adding and subtracting fractions with an addiction that made my brain thrum. The method—matching denominators, basic addition and subtraction of numerators, simplification—became instinct. It felt almost joyful to make numbers appear large—or, as Yeye put it, *ugly*—only to reduce them at the end to their true forms. 12/32 became 3/8. 14/35 became 2/5.

Grading my work, Yeye's eyes were downturned, his shriveled lips pushed out. Farsighted, he held the worksheet away from him. His chin became like the moon, craterous, and retreated into his neck. He moved his middle finger down the page and across as he reviewed.

"Good," he said, circling my grade at the top. He slid the worksheet to me. A tall skinny 100. "See? Who said you're bad at math."

His compliment kept me in a good mood until the evening, when my mother called me into her bedroom. I walked in just as she drew the last blind, twisting the stick that made the shades fold inward. When I got older, I would play moments like this in a sequence. Me entering her room, my mother engaged in some small task that announced her dominance over the space. Adjusting the mirrors that multiplied her presence. Closing the French doors to the bathroom behind her, glaring at me the whole time. And now, shutting out the night.

"Sit," she said. "How are your lessons going?"

"Okay." I knew she wanted something more precise, something quantitative, but I had learned from her how to withhold, the silent authority that came from keeping always a part of yourself, no matter how small, back.

She sat next to me on the bed and took out her hair clip. "You're lucky, you know. To have such a good teacher."

"Yeah, Dad told me."

My mother smiled, but her eyes didn't move. The goldfish did not appear. I brought my pinky up to my lips and began biting the skin around the nail, a habit I'd picked up recently. My mother knocked my hand away.

"I got a one hundred on a worksheet today," I said, caving. "And in the past week, my grades have all been in the nineties."

"That's not bad," she said. "There are still a few weeks before you test. Keep working hard and listening to Yeye."

"So what was it?" I asked.

"What was what?"

"The revolution in China."

The question sounded abrupt and strange even to me, though my thoughts must have been circling around this for at least the past month. I believe it was why I caused a scene at that dinner. It would be years before I realized that what I was asking about was her. As long as I accepted my mother as a mystery, I didn't wonder at her steely quiet. I might have never wondered, at least not for a long time, had Yeye not appeared in our lives.

She played with her clip in her lap, making the teeth open and close.

"It was a time that your father and I, and Ahyi, grew up in. The government was changing. Many people were afraid of intellectuals." She paused. "Do you know what *intellectual* means?"

She said the word in English. I did know, but I shook my head.

"It means highly educated. Someone devoted to their studies."

I joked, "Like me right now."

My mother stared me down, her big eyes dark and muted.

"During that period, anything anyone did that didn't praise

the new government was considered punishable. Books, music, art. History, too, because it held the country's past, which the government was trying to erase. You can see how it would be difficult for intellectuals, people whose lives were devoted to these subjects, to keep doing their work. But Yeye assumed he was safe. He came from a very brilliant, well-respected family, but he was a mathematician. He'd seen a few teachers from the wen hua department get carted away, but no one from his side.

"One morning he arrived at his office to find a poster on his door accusing him of hiding foreign documents. Officials searched his office and found letters written in English. Yeye explained that the letters were between him and a friend he'd made during his year abroad. They discussed ordinary things, mostly a way for him to practice his English. He told the officials to read the letters so they could see for themselves, but the officials were, like most people at the time, illiterate in English. They didn't appreciate what they thought was taunting. Yeye lost his position at the university over this and was forced to work as a janitor at a high school for many years before being allowed to return."

Her spine curled as her body softened. The bones in her back protruded like bolts, as though my mother were held together by metal.

She sat up. "You're fortunate, Eileen, not only to have such a wonderful teacher, but also to be able to study without worry or shame."

"What about my real grandparents?" I said, riding the excitement of the story. "Did they die in the revolution?"

My mother blinked twice. "You shouldn't talk of death like it's the easiest thing in the world." She stood and walked to the front of the room. She flicked the lights off, as though whatever she said next could only be heard in darkness. "No more questions. You won't fall asleep with such a full head."

The room was veiled in rose gold, the just-risen sun filtering through the humidity. It wasn't raining now, yet, but the forecast said sprinkles on and off for the next week. The rain was letting up. Autumn was moving in.

We practiced decimals. Lining up the dots for addition and subtraction. Counting the numbers behind the dot for multiplication and division. Converting into a fraction, a percentage. With the placement test approaching, our lessons had become mostly drills. Yeye gave me a geometry worksheet and left me alone to work while he smoked in the backyard.

In the past when he'd done this, I'd been impressed by his timing, how he never failed to lower himself into the chair, spreading his fresh tobacco scent just as I was completing the last problem. I'd made a game of trying to beat him, but even as I got faster, he seemed to anticipate my improvement. That, I thought, or his cigarettes kept getting shorter.

I boxed the last answer and waited for his return. When he wasn't back, I decided I would bring the worksheet to him. I walked to the back door of Ahyi's house, into the wonky rectangle of light on the linoleum kitchen floor, and saw Yeye's sandaled feet, tall white socks crossed right over left. I got closer until my nose was touching the glass.

The sky had lost its warmth in midmorning. It was pale blue, with clouds in lumpy, ragged sheets. I had planned on tapping the glass with my nail. Yeye was just to my right in a monobloc chair, but something about his posture—leaned back but rigid, eyes closed in a deliberate, unnatural way—stopped me. His left hand, the one holding the lit cigarette, was shaking a little, hovering above the chair arm. A cloud moved in front of the sun; it shadowed Yeye's face. I thought I saw that the corners of his eyes were wet, but seconds later, once the cloud had passed, his face was restored to its previous glow. Yeye opened his eyes directly to the sun. He brought the dying cigarette to his lips and pulled.

I walked back to the table and waited for him.

A week after I took the test, Yeye died in his sleep. Days later I found out that my score did not meet the mark, and I believe everyone was relieved that Yeye had been spared this final disappointment. The school year passed uneventfully, and the next summer and all the summers after that would return to the dry heat.

I'm able to recall that summer in detail, and I'm not sure if that should be attributed to the unusual weather or Yeye's presence. It's become a prophetic season in my mind, one in which it was determined that I would not lead an academic life. Benny would end up at Harvard. I would not.

My parents are in their sixties now. I recently turned thirty-five. I live in a college town not far from where I grew up. It was a job at the college that brought me back to Texas, after so many years away, and my mother's insistence that I be closer. In the intervening years, I'd accumulated my own heartaches, for which I suffered flagrantly. My family had watched me suffer, including Ahyi. She is retired now and comes to visit me every so often, making the two-hour drive.

We were sitting on my patio one morning, just the two of us, watching the day begin, when Yeye drifted into my thoughts. I had stopped thinking about him while I was absorbed in my own hardships. Now I returned to that summer. It was the first time I felt comfortable telling Ahyi what I knew, what my mother had told me. While I could never say that Ahyi and I were close before—our relationship through my mother something we'd both taken for granted—an ease had found its way into our dynamic, perhaps because she had seen me at my lowest. I was starting to consider her an older friend.

"How old were you then, eight?" she asked.

"Ten," I replied. "My father mentioned it, so I asked."

"If you've already heard the story, then what do you want to know?"

"You're his daughter," I said, as if that clarified anything.

I was about to retract my question by way of apology, ashamed for still coveting stories that did not belong to me. Then she began.

"It must have been the sixty-ninth year. Your mother and I were in eighth grade. We were best friends. Our families were close. People would call us 'Twins!' as if it were our names because we were together so often. We both joined the Red Successors so that when we reached high school, we would automatically become Red Guards. We were just kids. We wanted to be part of something.

"Things were starting to get extreme around that time. The movement was exciting—I don't know if you can understand. Your mother's parents ran a very successful tea parlor that had been the family business for generations. A beautiful space. Tall ceilings, the walls decorated with red paper cutouts that your grandmother created painstakingly, each one completely different, like snowflakes. Kids at school began picking on your mother. I remember one boy yelling in the hallway, *Your parents serve tea to rich pigs!* She was embarrassed and scared of losing her place in the Successors, so she tipped some of the Guards off about my father, your Yeye.

"I suppose she thought she was saving herself. She knew he had letters from the US because he'd used them to teach us English some evenings at our house. She would only tell me much later, when we were able to touch these old wounds without reopening them, that she figured they would knock him around a little and destroy the letters, but also that she couldn't say she was thinking much at all. She couldn't have guessed that the Red Guards, the oldest of them just seventeen, would come to our house at night and beat my parents in front of the town. Your

Yeye was punished not only for having the letters, but because—"

"They thought he was being arrogant when he asked them to read English," I said.

Ahyi nodded. "They left my father with two broken ribs, bleeding into the street. They kicked my mother's head until she was in a coma. You know all of this already?"

"Yes," I lied. "But continue, please."

"When my mother woke up, she couldn't speak or walk, the damage to her brain was so bad. She would be in a wheelchair the rest of her life. Your mother's plan backfired. The Guards, excited by their first big public beating, grew more aggressive. A week later, they barricaded your grandparents' tea parlor while your grandparents were still inside and burned the whole place to the ground. Your mother was in school when it happened. From anywhere in town you could smell the smoke.

"That night my father opened the front door and found your mother covered in soot, kneeling and touching her head to the ground. If anyone saw her, both she and Yeye would have been in trouble, as what she was doing was considered a feudal gesture, so Yeye pulled her inside, and that's when I saw her. 'Forgive me, forgive me!' she cried and cried. But I had sworn in my heart never to speak to her again, and I didn't think it was right to feel any differently simply because she was an orphan. I slapped her and told her to shut up. I struck her again and again until I was beating her with whatever part of my body I could. My father pulled me away.

"After that your mother lived with us. For the first year she and I did not speak. We established a routine, avoiding each other and taking turns caring for my disabled mother."

Ahyi began rubbing her knees, rocking a little backward and forward. I wondered if talking about this was causing her physical pain, but I didn't want her to stop.

"Forgiving her was the hardest thing I ever did," she said. "And I didn't do it out of nobility or a good heart like my father.

It's just what happened after enough time had passed. As an adult, your mother met a decent man, your father, and together they moved to the States. They sent money back to Yeye and me every month. My father, after he retired and was free to care for my mother full time, insisted that I move, too, so I did. Then my mother passed, and that's when you met Yeye."

She looked around, blinking. The day had grown light. Soon, the morning would be taken over by birds, and their song, as delicate as it was, would close the door on the careful quiet that roomed this conversation. I knew we might never open it again.

"What was it like once he returned to the university?" I asked, keeping my voice steady. "After the politics died down."

Ahyi stared in my general direction. "He was exonerated and permitted to return but didn't. The high school where he was a janitor was a short walk from our house. The hours were flexible. It was the easiest way to keep caring for my mother."

"And what about you?" I said to change the subject, in case she was beginning to suspect what I knew. "How come you never got married?"

"I could ask you the same thing. Even our naughty Benny found a wife! Why haven't you found a husband?"

"I'm young still by today's standards."

"Today's standards, yesterday's standards. After thirty, it's all the same to men. There's a saying that goes *Better luck finding pure gold than a perfect man*. I decided long ago that it would be better to skip the man, go straight for the gold with those odds!"

She was in a jokey mood, as she often was these days, retaining that upbeat quality she'd always had but with a softer touch. Or it's possible I'm the one who changed. When I was old enough to care, I learned that Ahyi was more successful than my parents, who'd both worked in computer software. Ahyi had been a real estate agent. Toward the end of her career she was mostly selling to millionaires in California who viewed Texas as the next frontier. How different she seemed now from that intimidating, efficient woman I'd grown up watching.

That night, I had trouble falling asleep. I thought about calling Benny but wondered if a call that late would worry him, coming from me. Years ago, in my twenties, I wanted to die because a man I loved had left me for another. The second time I woke up in the hospital, my mother was there. The goldfish beneath her eyes had set, I noticed, and I wondered when that had happened. She got into the small bed with me and bowed my head to her chest. It's one of the only times I can remember us touching.

"Is this the worst you've ever felt?" I asked.

"Yes," she'd said. "Yes."

Compromise

My name is Sui and in June I'll be turning sixty. I have three adult children; their names are Charlotte, Pam, and David. My husband died in October, while the leaves were still green and clinging to their branches. Now it is spring and there are new leaves, and I am a widow. Such are the major facts of my life.

I live alone in the house my husband left me. I work as the secretary at Royal Dental on Lamar Boulevard, a job I've had for about as long as I've been in the US, long enough to watch the practice pass from Dr. Baker, the original proprietor, to his son. I take in the mail and water my plants. On weekends I prepare a meal whenever I get hungry, which is sometimes twice and sometimes four times a day, indulging a little in the absence of structure. I talk to my children on the phone whenever one of them thinks to call. I say hello to my neighbors, who are comforting to me in the same way that my house is, as guideposts in time, reminding me of who I am. I have known most of them for over twenty years. They're the closest I have to friends. When I wave to them from across our yards, I think how lucky I am to be standing at a distance, oblivious to the details of their lives, how they move inside their homes, and to not have to see their faces up close. A person's face is like a house, I think. The marks and stains and sunken places are proof of what has happened, but they cannot tell the whole story.

Even before my husband died, I was treated like a widow. That was eighteen years ago, when he left. I was not young, but I was younger. My neighbors are Christians. Most of them go to Hill County Bible just a couple miles down the road, next to the Korean grocery store where I like to buy fruit. They brought casseroles and brownies to my doorstep, sending their small children sometimes for extra sweetness, and I was not charmed or annoyed by this so much as I was amused. When Mrs. Wilhite, the very old preacher's very old wife, had asked me on the sidewalk one evening how my husband was, only a week after Huayu told me he was staying in Beijing—he wasn't coming back, I'd told her the truth, because I saw no reason not to. "He's gone," I'd said. Her blue eyes bulged out of her powdered white face. "Another woman," I explained. "In China," I added, to calm any questions about who she might be. "*Affair,*" I said slowly. It was an English word I'd practiced for the sole purpose of explaining my situation.

Back then, David was only five and running around in his underwear, aiming dart guns at his older sisters. Now he's a year out of college. I don't know much about the Christian faith, but I do know something about people, and I think they treated me like a widow in order to preserve my dignity, because out of the myriad ways to experience loss, death is by far the noblest. A month after I told Mrs. Wilhite the news, she showed up at my doorstep holding an envelope. By this point the gifts and pasta salads and people "just checking up on me" had subsided somewhat. "For you," she'd said. "From the congregation." Inside were ten one-hundred-dollar bills. "Just something to tide you over." I took the money. Why not? As the Americans say, I had three mouths to feed. I traced the lines in Mrs. Wilhite's face, moving from her eyes down to her pink neck. Then she said, "She wong," and it was like when I'd said *affair*, it sounded tentative. *Xi wang*. Hope. "She wong," she said again, just before turning to leave.

Mrs. Wilhite has since passed away and so has her husband, the preacher. They weren't alive to witness my husband's return—his rebirth, one might say—this past fall. He had pancreatic cancer. My sister-in-law called me from Beijing in July, just after I turned fifty-nine, and I had to ask her to repeat her name, it'd been so long since I'd heard from her. She claimed that hospice care was better in the US than in China, and I didn't ask about the other woman, the one he'd left us for all those years ago. Instead I asked how much time. "The doctors say half a year," she said, her words choppy over the phone. Later, when I told my kids, they warned me that it could end up being much longer than that. They said these things are unpredictable, and you never know when someone might live longer than expected, although in my husband's case it ended up being shorter. When I didn't respond, my sister-in-law said, "He's still his children's father." She whispered it, like it was a secret. Like I didn't know. "They should see him before he goes, right?"

I didn't tell her that my children hated their father, and that to them hate was as much a virtue as love. They called the idea "absurd" and "unfair," and for the three months that Huayu lived here in his old home, Pam was the only one who visited.

"The others don't know I'm here," she said after I swung open the front door. I'd thought it was going to be the nurse, Toby. She stepped around me to get inside. When had she arrived in town? I wondered. And how long was she planning on staying? What made her decide to come? I stayed standing with the door wide open, blinking at the street. It was September, and the weather was sunny and mild with a delicious breeze. My neighbor saw me and waved. I waved back.

"Is that him?"

I closed the door. She gestured with her head at the bed in the living room, which sat facing the windows to the backyard. The blinds were drawn. It was afternoon and dark in the house. Who else could it be? Huayu was asleep. I realized that I was more nervous for Pam than I had been for myself. When I saw Huayu in the airport for the first time in almost two decades, it was as I had predicted—shocking, not because he was someone I once knew, but because he was a person I did not recognize. The sickness had altered him. It was like receiving a new man, a new husband, and to me this was a relief. I'd agreed to do this because I know that death is the greatest simplifier. It covers up old wounds, which is basically as good as healing them. At the airport a woman in a vest was pushing Huayu in a wheelchair. I spotted him not by searching for my husband but by searching for anybody who looked sick. Then he pointed at me, and it made me wonder what he'd been looking for, what gave me away. He was amazingly thin. His hair was white and sparsely laid. His coat was a gray shell, and he curled himself deep into it, the flesh around his mouth and eyes like wax that had dripped and hardened again.

I followed Pam to Huayu's bedside. The living room had remained unchanged, aside from the bed and the PCA machine, which was connected to the IV in Huayu's hand. I tried to recall the last time Pam was here. My kids have stopped coming home for the holidays. They prefer going to Charlotte's in California, and I can't complain because they always buy my plane ticket. It was only some years ago, I remembered, when David graduated from high school. There was still the brown leather couch and the matching one-seater. The same glass coffee table. Pam looked down at her father's sleeping face, the jowly skin. "How dare you come back to us," she said, like she was reciting a fact. I watched them from behind the headboard. Huayu's mouth was open. His breaths were strained, as though the air were passing through a grated barrier. "How dare you come back to us like this."

She stayed looking at her father until the hum of the machine grew loud, the chirping of his vitals sucking up the quiet in the house like insects in the night.

"He won't wake for a while," I said, to break the noise. Of course, now I wish I'd said something else, something that would have validated what Pam was feeling, even though she didn't understand that her father could only come back like this, only with death as the circumstance. "The morphine puts him into a very deep sleep."

It turned out that Pam was only staying for one night, and even so, she booked a hotel. "I changed my mind, I don't want to be here when he's up," she said once we were back outside. In the sunlight, her hair took on a matted sheen. I noticed that her face looked sharper, like someone had pinched her jaw toward the tip of her chin. She'd lost weight. Or maybe she was just getting older. "I mostly wanted to check on you anyway. I fly back in the morning."

"You're sure you don't want to talk to him?" I said. I thought that she should, if only to save herself from regret in the future.

"Don't tell Charlotte and David I came. I'll tell them myself later."

"I won't," I said.

"Don't tell him I came either."

At this I felt myself frown, but I promised.

It is astounding to me how my children have turned out. I suppose it is always this way between children and parents. Charlotte, for example, my oldest, has a completely different view of our neighbors. "They were trying to convert us, obviously," she said at the table one night during Christmas dinner. This was some years ago, when David was still in high school. We were at my house, which I still thought of then as mine and theirs. A discussion about capitalism and Christmas, which we only ever celebrated secularly, had turned into a discussion about religion. I could hardly keep up.

"Was it obvious?" I said.

Charlotte had prepared steaks on the grill, and I'd asked for mine well done and was having a hard time cutting into it. Only in Texas was it warm enough to grill outside in December. David had asked for his medium rare and was using the blood on his plate as a sauce, swirling his fork around in it to wet every bite.

"They gave us a thousand dollars," said Charlotte. "No one does that without expecting something in return."

She worked her fork and knife against the meat with great precision.

I didn't tell them that nobody—not Mrs. Wilhite or her husband or anybody from Hill County Bible who stopped at my house during that month—ever asked me if I would like to join the church. Charlotte would've just said that the money was invitation enough. She'd grown suspicious of people, and who could blame her? She was sixteen when her father left.

Pam reached for her wine. Pam is a vegetarian and was eating a medley of root vegetables, carrots and daikon and beets. "I don't remember any of this at all," said David with his mouth full, and then the conversation moved on to something else.

In the three months we spent together, Huayu never asked if the children were coming to see him. I think he was afraid of the answer. "A real musician," he said once, after I told him that Pam plays the cello in the Berlin Philharmonic. This was before she visited. "She wasn't even playing the instrument full size when—" He coughed, an unwieldy sound, like the top notes of metal slicing into metal, and he never returned to that thought.

Was it awkward between us? My children asked me this over Thanksgiving at Charlotte's, a month after their father had passed. I told them it wasn't. "But how could it not be?" said David. The four of us were sitting on Charlotte's couch, drinking chrysanthemum tea. "Did he at least say he was sorry?"

Their mugs were paused in midair while they waited for an answer, hovering around their necks, and the synchronicity made them appear momentarily childlike. When they were little, I had gotten used to things happening in threes. It happened despite the age gap between the girls and David. Three people tying their shoes. Three people throwing rocks in a lake, three plunks as the rocks struck water. A few times the occurrences were more eerie. Three people scratching an itch that happened to be in the exact same place on three separate bodies. Perhaps it was this maternal omniscience, felt rarely now, the ability to see them as they could not see themselves, that empowered me to say what I said next.

"There was a funeral at the church."

I took a sip of my tea. It burned my tongue. Pam set her mug on the end table. "Some of the neighbors still remembered him. He was baptized."

"They'll do anything to take part in another person's misery," Charlotte scoffed.

"He was in a lot of pain at the end."

"He made choices," said Charlotte. Her voice was loud, and it reminded me that I was dealing with adults. "He isn't redeemed just because he got sick." She spoke of redemption with such confidence for someone who doesn't believe in religion. Again I was astounded. Where did my children get these ideas?

"Did he apologize?" said David.

My son never really knew his father, doesn't have clear memories of him. Does that give him more to begrudge or less?

I said, "Yes. He did."

I lied to my children that night, and it was not the only lie I told over the entire ordeal. There had been an unspoken agreement between me and Huayu that we would not discuss his eighteen-year absence. With those years struck from our history, there was nothing to be sorry for. I was the one feeding him and washing him, and later, dispensing his medicine to relieve his pain. If I wanted to talk about it at any time, he would've had no choice but to listen, being as he was captive to these needs and therefore captive to me. But I wasn't interested in moving backward in that direction.

At first we didn't talk at all. To Toby, the nurse who came by every Monday and Thursday, it probably looked normal enough, like one of those marriages where the talking had petered out and now companionship functioned best without it. Then one day I was giving Huayu a bath using a washcloth and a basin of warm water. We were three weeks in. I was taking leave from work indefinitely, having been guaranteed my job back whenever I wanted it. A gift from the Baker family, the young Dr. Baker had expressed demurely the last time I was in the office, for my thirty years of service to him and his father. The dentists are Christians as well; there's a decal on the waiting room wall, a quote from Corinthians that says, "Love never ends. But as for prophecies, they will come to an end; as for tongues, they will cease; as for knowledge, it will come to an end," which I've always found harsh for a dentist's office. I figured the Bakers' generosity had to do with their being afraid of death and not wanting to play a role in hastening it. Huayu was lying on his side so that I could do his back, where the skin was looser than it was on his arms and legs. It bunched as I dragged the cloth across, reminding me of the film that forms on top of cooling rice porridge. A faulty cover for what lies underneath.

He said, "That stain."

There were holes in his voice. I wrung the cloth into the basin and looked at where he was pointing, at a corner of the ceiling above the couch.

"That wasn't there when I left."

Somehow the stain, which looked like a brown storm cloud, bridged the gap between his leaving and coming back. Perhaps Huayu had been trying to make himself vulnerable, give me the opening for the conversation he thought I wished to have, but his acknowledgment was enough for me.

We talked a little more after that, usually when I was bathing him or spooning rice porridge into his mouth. I told him the facts of his children's lives, like what each of them does for work, but I did not delve into the truer qualities that make them who they are, that make them real and foreign to me. I stayed with my children and yet I don't fully know them, so I could only imagine how it might feel to suddenly see Charlotte, Pam, and David as people with attitudes and tastes.

We took a vacation to Port Aransas once when it was the five of us. The beach stretched for miles and miles. The tide rolled back, and the wet sand caught the light from the sky and made a glowing path on the ground. Huayu asked the kids to build a sandcastle. David was a toddler and couldn't be bothered with anything beyond sensation. He flapped his arms as the tide came in and water frothed between his little legs. Charlotte was fourteen and serious. She packed sand into pails and turned the pails upside down, patting them all around so that the shapes came out whole. When they didn't, or when a piece fell off later, she started over. Pam, who was nine, couldn't match Charlotte's intensity for the project, so she eventually wandered off on her own, collecting shells. Huayu and Charlotte worked for hours. Focused and quick, Charlotte was the perfect fit for Huayu, to impress him, even though he'd wanted his firstborn to be a son. I watched them while keeping an eye on the other two, occasionally offering someone a piece of fruit. They crawled on all fours and kneeled, etching ridges in the castle walls. They dug a moat around the four towers and filled it up with water.

My children think it was a kindness that bordered on

stupidity—one that resembles martyrdom—that allowed me to take care of their father, my husband, when really it had nothing to do with kindness at all. We get so few chances in life to be of real use to another person, to make their life more bearable, and meanwhile the chances to do harm are everywhere and often discreet; you don't fully realize what you've done until it's over. My kids are somewhat estranged from me now because they don't understand. It is my hope that they will always be clear-sighted regarding what's right and wrong, so that their lives will remain straightforward.

Charlotte hates her father even now, even though he's dead. I never told him how she felt, partly to spare him and partly because I was jealous. I don't think any of my children find me worthy of such strong emotion, not even Pam, who came to me in Charlotte's guest room the night I lied to them over tea. She apologized on her sister's behalf, and I thought of that day on the beach, when she had drifted off by herself.

"She's not angry at you," Pam said. "She's angry at him."

"I'm actually fine with the fact that he left, to be honest," she said when I didn't respond. We were sitting at the edge of the bed. The lights were off in the room but there were no blinds or curtains on any of the windows in Charlotte's house. Cold light from the street came pouring in, casting shadows across Pam's face. "What I'll never understand is why he had to cut us off completely. He didn't visit once. All those years, I kept wondering whether he thought about us. Whether or not he missed me."

My children had all been looking to me to match them in some way, Charlotte her anger, David his confusion, to reflect what they felt back to them. Pam was devastated, maybe more so because she had seen her father. She wanted me to be too, but I knew my own devastation couldn't console her.

"People deal with things in the way they know how," I said,

reaching for something solid. "He had the decency at least to tell us the truth about why he was leaving. He gave us the house."

Pam smiled. "You know, Mom, sometimes I think you're a good person, but then I think you have no standards for people at all, and what good is that?" She stood up from the bed and said good night. She shut my door gently, and then I was alone.

Pam's surprise visit came at the six-week mark, right in the middle of Huayu's stay. I remember it wasn't long afterward that he asked the question I believe he'd been building up to ever since he pointed out that stain. Recently, a maintenance person came by and said the stain was a result of condensation in the attic. The old pipes have since been replaced, but I've decided to leave the stain, to not paint over it.

I was telling Huayu about David. "He's been into lifting weights. He's trying to get his sisters into it, too." Was this awkward? Maybe this was what my children had meant, but to me it felt easy, like talking to a stranger or myself. Huayu accepted it like a stranger, with detached interest, nodding and swallowing his porridge. I scraped the bowl to collect the dregs, the sticky white starch. By this point his pain had gotten worse, and Toby had just upped his dosage. Some liquid leaked out of the corner of Huayu's mouth. I caught it with the spoon.

"I want to ask you something," he said. "You might find it strange."

I feared he was going to ask about the kids, about why they hadn't come to see him. I set the bowl down on the counter behind me. He picked up the morphine pump, holding it loosely as though it were a candy bar or a TV remote. It was a simple handheld device, gray with a green button on top.

"I hate this," he said, "having to do this for myself. I'm wondering if you would be willing to do it for me. Push the button."

What he was asking of me was forbidden, and I said so.

Toby had said only the patient was allowed to administer his own morphine.

"Who will know?" said Huayu. "In return, I'll give you something as well."

I laughed, quietly to myself at first but then I couldn't stop. What could he give me in his current condition? The laugh came from the bottom of my stomach. I threw my head back and let the sound hit the walls. It spread throughout the house.

"I'll listen," he said after I was done. "I'll listen to whatever you have to say, whatever you want to tell me."

I felt exposed all of a sudden, defensive. "What is this? Some kind of deal?"

"Not a deal, an exchange."

"What could I possibly have to tell you?" I said, even though by then I must have already been thinking about his offer, accepting it. Some part of me wonders whether I had planned this moment all along.

"Everyone has stories they've kept to themselves."

"And why would I tell you?" My heart was pounding.

"Because I'll be dead soon."

He let go of the device. He brushed his knuckles briefly against mine before letting his arm flop back onto the bed, hardly making a sound.

"Whatever judgments I have, I'll take them with me."

Our time together had been a careful game, where all the pieces were things left unspoken. The children. The absence. He'd broken an essential rule. It was as though glass had shattered on the floor.

"You don't know how much time you have," I said, staring out the window. I was startled by his touch. I'd stopped raising the blinds as often after the pain increased and Huayu fell into a more or less permanent fatigue, but Toby said even a few minutes of sunshine each day could be beneficial. The grass was yellow, the day was overcast and bright. Birds hopped along the fence between my backyard and my neighbor's.

Huayu said, "I can feel it."

When I lived in Beijing and attended university, I fell in love with my best friend's fiancé. "He might have loved me too," I said to Huayu. "No matter what we tried, we couldn't stop seeing each other."

This was days later, after I'd had time to think. I was sitting in a chair next to the bed, between the bed and the old coffee table. We kept our gazes forward. I was holding the device, and it felt solid in my grip, even as my palm began to sweat. Through the window from outside, we might have looked like a couple admiring the view, but the blinds were closed, and even though Huayu was awake, I chose not to open them.

The dark house created a sense of timelessness. Days began to blur. I told my husband bits and pieces until eventually he had the whole story.

Stripped to its bones, my story is ordinary. The guilt over the affair was painful but I couldn't stop, so eventually I dropped out of school. I married a man, Huayu, who took me to the States, where I could count on never seeing my friend again.

"Did you ever think about just being together?" Huayu asked. This was toward the end. A week later I would walk into the living room to find my husband stiff and slack-jawed, not breathing. He'd called me over to do the button. I held it down with my thumb. There was an ease between us now that wasn't there before, when I was filling his head with my children's hobbies and credentials. I lowered myself into the chair next to him.

"He suggested it once. I said no. What we were doing was wrong, but in my mind it was not as wrong as openly breaking an innocent person's heart."

"She would have forgiven you eventually."

"What makes you so sure?"

He didn't answer. Then he said, "Why did you let me come back?"

"Not because I forgive you," I said, and I told him what I thought about death, how it is its own morality and doesn't have to compromise with whatever one's life has been. Something about that had always attracted me. "You can say no to love," I said to him, looking at him. "You can't say no to death."

Huayu nodded. "A simple morality."

"And pure," I said.

"What if I asked you to forgive me?" said Huayu. "What if I told you a story from my life? Would you have sympathy?"

The morphine was working. He was struggling to stay awake.

"That wasn't part of our deal. Besides, it's not my place to forgive you, just like it's not your place to forgive me."

"Whose place is it to forgive you?"

"My friend," I said, "whom I betrayed and then abandoned."

"And me?" he said.

I sighed. "Our children, but none of them want to see you."

I considered telling him about Pam, how she'd flown all the way from Berlin just to say two sentences to him while he was asleep. He could count that as forgiveness. But my loyalties were to her, I'd promised her, so in the end I stuck with my lie.

"I want to be baptized," he said. "Before I die, I want to be forgiven."

"I'll arrange it," I said, feeling as though we were always headed here, like we had finally arrived.

A crew came by to pick up the equipment. The bed, the machines, the various cords that connected to various ports, all taken apart and packed into a van returning to the hospital. Toby was there. I realized I would not be seeing him anymore, and I felt a small shock in my heart, like I would miss him, even though that was ridiculous. I think a lot about meeting Toby. In my house that first day, he'd placed an IV in Huayu's hand. He connected the PCA tubing to the morphine and attached the maintenance fluids through the Y-port—explaining each action as he did it in a kind of running narration. For whose benefit, this wasn't clear. There was a melody to it though, which made it nice to listen to. The liquid moved in spurts down the tube and disappeared into Huayu's hand.

Toby was a good nurse, but he'll fade from my memory eventually, just as more important people in my life have. But I'll never forget what he said.

I was showing him to the door. "How long was the flight from Beijing?" he asked.

"About fifteen hours." Doctors had approved the flight, but suddenly I was worried. I asked if it was bad.

"No, no," said Toby. "The cancer has done its damage. There's not much that can make it worse." He looked back at my husband, even though from where we were by the door, you could only see the headboard.

"It's painful, that's all." He stared into my eyes. "It's a terribly long time to be in pain."

After my living room was restored, Toby said goodbye and that he was sorry for my loss. I told him thank you. He's a kind person, just like the young female pastor who dabbed water on Huayu's forehead, and like my employers the Dr. Bakers and my neighbors, who brought all kinds of gifts and flowers after my husband died for real this time and also attended his funeral at the end of October, when the leaves were crisp and finally falling.

In June, I'll be sixty. I'll have been a widow for eight months, but it already feels like much longer.

Acknowledgments

I am grateful to the Iowa Writers' Workshop and the Richard E. Guthrie Memorial Fellowship for generous support while I was writing this book. Sasha Khmelnik, Deb West, Jan Zenisek, Connie Brothers, and Jane Van Voorhis are indispensable to the program at Iowa and made my time there special. Thank you to the New York State Summer Writers Institute, the Sun Valley Writers' Conference, and the Ragdale Foundation for teaching, feeding, and housing me at various points.

To my agent, David McCormick, who always responds to my emails cheerfully—I am glad we met. I can't imagine someone caring for these stories as well as you have.

Anyone who knows my editor knows she is a genius. Thank you, Brigid Hughes, for inhabiting these stories so deeply and asking questions I will be thinking about for a long time. And for everything you do for literature.

Megan Cummins and Ruby Wang at A Public Space, for ensuring my book's safe passage into the world. Janet Hansen, for the thoughtful cover and design.

I have had remarkable teachers. Yiyun Li's writing and insights have changed how I think about storytelling and what language makes possible. Jess Walter, Ethan Canin, Charles D'Ambrosio, and Margot Livesey—I could never say thank you enough. Your fingerprints mark these stories.

My friends—Natasha Chernis, Laura Seiger, Brigitte Levea, Ryan Whittington, Emily Delacruz, Alisa Guardiola, Shirin Amlani, Damian Miller, Rob Lau, Kha Phi, Eliza Berkowitz, Mel Maxwell, Christina Pulles, Mo Mundy, Hanna Otero, Zaneta Jung, Brett Duquette, Chris Schwartz, Jess Minhas, Ian Evans, Vernon Caldwell, Sri Rao, Seiji Carpenter, Chloe Chang, Steve Juh, Andy Gupta, Lina Moysis, Bao-Tran Huynh, Abigail Carney, Matthew Kelly, Santiago Sanchez, Karen Nicoletti, Peter Lessler, Arinze Ifeakandu, Esther Okonkwo, Jing Jian, Meg Frietag, Aaron Hwang, Belinda Huijuan Tang, IfeOluwa Nihinlola, Jeff Boyd, You Jin Lee, Shaquille Brissett, Kenneth Ibegwam, Alexa Frank, and others—I cherish you all. My warmest appreciation for Kristin Gilliard, Alonzo Vereen, Natalia Majette, Janak Ramakrishnan, Jamel Brinkley, and Lucy Tan, who are family to me.

Arna Bontemps Hemenway—thanks for holding me accountable to what we do. No one has changed my life quite like you have, in part by introducing me to Lan Samantha Chang, who has done more for my writing than anyone.

I would not have survived childhood without my brother, Jonathan Zhang. Endless gratitude to my parents, Airong Zhang and Zhiyu Zhang, for loving me.

Ada Zhang

is a graduate of the Iowa Writers' Workshop. Her short stories have appeared in *A Public Space*, *McSweeney's*, *American Short Fiction*, and elsewhere. She grew up in Austin, Texas, and now lives in New York City. *The Sorrows of Others* is her first book.